Almost Southern
Stories from
Marsden

Dennis Sinar

Almost Southern

DEDICATION

To Kathryn

Contents

ACKNOWLEDGMENTS

The inspiration for the fictional town of Marsden comes from familiar places I've visited, but there is no intent to link these stories to a person or an event in any of those places. Extensive notes, listening, and merging life situations with multiple personalities provides the content. Sincere thanks to members of the Writer's Block for their encouragement and critique to make these stories stronger. Special thanks to Barbara Rouse for her support and humor and for always being willing to read another story. I appreciate readers Shawn Riley and Marni Graff for their reviews, Philip Hamrick for his helpful insights on the story "At the end of the hall" and Bubba Rowlett and Trisha Johnston for their input. Thanks to Nancy Faussett for her passion about the correct tense. These stories are better because Dean Sutzer promoted mindfulness. The editing of Tia Bach corrected my errors and any that remain are from my late changes. Thanks to my wife Kathryn for reading, laughing and pointing out inconsistencies and especially for tolerating my daydreaming about the characters and their lives.

THE BUM

Overnight I had become a bum. I'd never really intended such a fall, but in retirement, it's easy to slide down that slippery slope to bum-ness. The transformation started during the first week of January, a time of unusual winter cold in Marsden. The Christmas hubbub was over and there was nothing to look forward to during the long cold spell. Persistent wet cold paralyzed me more than snow or gray overcast skies. The warming days of March were in the distant future.

Each morning for the past two weeks, I awoke without motivation. There was cold and dark outside my window at bedtime and the same cold and dark half a day later as I rushed from the warmth of my thick covers to the heated blanket in my easy chair. Patrice is heat conservative and makes comments like "Propane prices just went up," "you can always put on more clothes," and especially poignant, "you need to get more circulation through your skin, so get up from that chair and do something. You're becoming a bum." Her comments pass unheeded through one cold ear and out the other. A warm blanket, a cozy chair, and a cup of warm tea are the daily comforts in my world. To me, a bum is a shiftless lackadaisical character, more of a loveable loafer. Cold weather turns me into that loveable loafer.

Patrice is too good a wife to believe I'm a bum, but I know that's what she's thinking. Over the past cold weeks, my retirement activity had temporarily stagnated — I was doing nothing. As can happen to retirees during down times, a comfortable routine settles in and now waiting for the next meal while sitting in my recliner is the highpoint of the day. Patrice serves breakfast and lunch on a regular schedule; I eat on a tray propped between the arms of the chair. After a mid afternoon nap, I enjoy a happy hour with wine and snacks in late afternoon followed by dinner in front of the television, then a small dessert, some light reading in my recliner, and back to my warm bed. I've repeated the pattern over the past weeks with minor variations. Events in the world pass by, ignored.

My personal hygiene has slipped as well, but I do not count that as unusual. My justification is that I am rebelling against twenty years of the daily monotony of meetings and the uniform of work: heavily starched shirt, suit coat, fashionable tie, and shined shoes. Now, in my golden years, there is no reason to shower, shave, get dressed, or even move much. I've earned the freedom to be lazy. If I don't look in the mirror and don't leave the house, my world is circumscribed to everything it needs to be. Why should I get cleaned up or change clothes? It is only Patrice who sees me.

As I've mentioned before, Patrice is an excellent wife, a gem who puts up with much of my nonsense without comment. She is tolerant, supportive, and gentle in her feedback. Lately, it appears as if I've violated even her tolerance level. She dropped gentle hints at first; things like "I really like to see you spiffed up in the morning" or "You look so good with your hair combed and a fresh shave." Another favorite: "I went shopping yesterday and got this wonderful blue shirt that pulls out the color of your eyes. I wonder if you could try it on." Yet another approach, "I'm going grocery shopping and maybe we could go to the city and have a nice lunch together?" All gentle comments, not inflammatory and not one of them refer to my being a bum.

I have an unusual talent of developing witty phrases and the talent has grown in retirement. The abundance of rest and good food has made clever, witty phrases appear like a cartoon bubble above my head, effortlessly floating above the comfort of my warm recliner. A recent witticism:

> The longer one appears to be a bum, the more like a bum one becomes. Being a bum is self-fulfilling.

I'll have to rework it to make it a little tighter, but it's a keeper for sure. I haven't told Patrice yet, but about 1:30 each afternoon, after my nap, I make notes in my pocket notebook of clever comments, funny sayings that I think about during the day. Witty words or phrases just seem to appear in that bubble over my head and I chuckle out loud at the good ones. Such gems need to be saved in my notebook. Right now, I can't think of any witty phrases except the bum one, but I'm sure I have plenty in the notebook that can be polished for later use.

My being a bum has contaminated Patrice's life as well. She goes out less with her friends, emails less, and has pretty much isolated herself from the outside. Notably, dinner is less often home cooked and more often processed food heated in the microwave. The other day she asked me to go down to the freezer and choose whatever I wanted for dinner. Inside there were stacked shelves of prepared foods, some of them with bright orange sale tags marking proximity to an expiration date. Patrice is the consummate thrifty wife.

I didn't have any complaints about the choices: usually Asian, Italian, or vegetarian. I'm glad she gives me responsibility for dinner because I can count the walk up and down the stairs as exercise and exercise occasionally stimulates a witty phrase. On this night, an Asian package close to the front looked appealing. The package said it was a restaurant-quality dinner for two prepared in a single pan on the stovetop within ten minutes. I've developed a hankering for Asian food, especially a restaurant-quality entree. As I came up the stairs, I noticed that Patrice was setting out paper plates, plastic ware, and paper napkins on my tray. I put the frozen package on the counter, poured a glass of wine, and went back to my cozy chair to wait for dinner. Shortly after I sat down, another witty comment came to mind.

> A great wife gently helps you over life's bumps but doesn't push you over them.

Gold, pure gold.

Unfortunately, my bum's life will have to end. Tomorrow is Tuesday, my day to wheel the garbage cans to the curb and clean the bathrooms. After that kind of activity, it's hard to go back to a bum's life.

JULESKY'S

The worn sign above the door told all that needed to be told.

Julesky's - Still Offering Useful Items after 60 years

A trial of any item is available at a low cost

Patrice had given Roger the challenge of finding an antique juice squeezer. Her grandmother had a metal one and the juice tasted so good; she could not get the memory out of her head. He suspected the challenge was as much to get him out of the house, as it was to start on her latest health quest of fresh juice each morning.

Where to find an antique juice squeezer? His breakfast buddies at the Mecca Grill sent him to Julesky's, a worn building at the far end of Hamilton Street where the pavement met the gravel road. It was a can't-miss-it type of building. The sign above the door was obvious, as was the junk scattered in the front yard and around the building.

When old man Julesky bought the lot in the 1950s, it was the cheapest lot in town and the end of civilization, separating the town of Marsden from the countryside. As Roger walked through the front door, he saw tall wooden shelves packed with stuff touching the ceiling. Items were arranged as if they'd been thrown from the center of the room and sat where they landed, most dangling off the ledge. Further into the room, there was a cluttered cluster of wooden and metal chairs circling a wood stove with a tall blackened chimney flue that disappeared through the ceiling. Julesky's was the meeting place where every morning at nine the oldest guys in town dissected the news of the day—the most informative stop on the circuit—before heading home for a late morning nap. When a person left Julesky's, they knew all the news and what everyone thought of it.

Old Julesky died in the store three years before; keeled over next to his chair just after opening for business. As a memorial, his cane was bolted to the right arm of the pale blue metal chair at the head of the circle. Julesky Junior, thereafter called JJ, stepped into his father's shoes, and claimed his chair the day after the funeral. JJ pushed the business into the modern world by posting a sign that advertised free Wi-Fi. Not that the sign mattered, because none of the old guys used a computer, but he thought it was progressive. JJ expanded the storage space and inventory by piling even more items a shelf higher and adding a covered roof. If an item was to be had in Marsden, someone could find it on one of the shelves.

As Roger roamed from room to room, he knew there would be an antique juice squeezer. There were tools, furniture, bathroom stalls, kitchen items, and vintage books arranged according to a filing system the Julesky family had used for years. If a customer wanted an antique decorative Pepsi-Cola sign without rust, JJ would send him to building three, left side, toward the back to find the sign hanging low on the wall. He advised the customer not to touch it, as the sign might very well drop and the resulting dent would make it worth less. Before the customer left the front counter, she knew the sign was twenty-five dollars, take it, or leave it. Everyone knew to yell if they needed help, and JJ or one of his staff would be along shortly to answer questions. There were too many items to price individually, so there was plenty of work for the staff answering questions.

All the locals sold their junk to old Julesky when he was alive, and then to JJ as people came to trust him. For useful items in good condition, JJ would pay a few dollars more than the pawnshop, and the inventory was a step above what people might throw to the curb. For example, a family might find a Monopoly board game missing a few pieces and might already have the missing pieces and the match gave them a complete game, cheap. There was a section in the back room devoted to gadgets once advertised on TV - plastic containers that cooked pasta in less than two minutes or a machine that sewed buttons onto shirts. There were containers of creams, balms, and perfumes tested by former owners and mostly full that were filed in room two on shelves at shoulder height.

The changing stock was why most people liked the store; the kind of place one could wander on a rainy afternoon. Julesky's was an island of nostalgia in a changing world. If you lived in Marsden and JJ knew you, he would let you try an item at home for a day or two for a dollar. JJ was a businessman like his father, the price he told you was the final price, no haggling and no whining. As he wandered from room to room, Roger spotted treasures that he'd always wanted but had never gotten around to buying. He had a weakness for cleaning products and stain removers for stubborn stains. After thirty minutes of browsing in room three, top shelf, middle, he found two orange juice squeezers JJ said were there; one in better condition than the other because the handle was not bent.

The liveliest spot in the store on any day, and at any time, was the center section of the main room. The regular gossips sat in a circle in their usual chairs, feet propped against the unlit stove and waited for their turn at the discussion. Even with the cold stove, there was a plenty of hot air coming from the group and it was blown around the room by an oscillating fan on a tall rusted stand.

June 14, 2013, about 10:00 AM, turned out to be the most memorable day at Julesky's that anyone had ever known. Clifton Peny was telling the story about his worthless son, a story everyone had heard at least twice, when he stopped midsentence and turned to face the young man who had just walked through the front door. The man advanced to the circle of friends holding a shiny gun and he pointed it around the circle. He wanted all their money. As events unfolded in the next minute, the gunman watched each man's face turn from disbelief to fear, as they looked right and left around the circle for directions on what to do.

Everyone around the circle noticed that the hammer was cocked on the firearm and it was ready to fire. The young man wore no mask and everyone knew that the family lived on the opposite side of town. Clifton later recalled his name as Curt something. To the men around the circle, he seemed inexperienced as a robber. His hands shook as he waved the gun around the group and Amos Roosevelt thought he might blow their heads off from pure nervousness. JJ stood beside his dad's chair and faced the young man, careful to keep his hands visible.

"Now, son, we know you're one of us. By the way you're acting, some bad trouble must be bearing down on you. We can all relate to bad trouble. We've all had our share, and we've gotten through it. How about you set down that gun before you hurt somebody, and let's talk? I'm sure we'll be able to come up with a solution without involving the police. You've seen enough reports on the news lately to know that when guns are involved, the police too often come in shooting. The guy holding the gun never fares well."

The young man nodded, but gave no indication of putting down the shiny gun.

"Son," JJ continued, "none of us wants an unexpected discharge, so can you at least uncock the hammer and take your finger off the trigger? That would make our talking a bit easier and ease up on some nervousness."

Everyone nodded agreement but moved to the edge of their chairs, ready to dive for cover just in case. The young man nodded again, uncocked the hammer, and eased his finger off the trigger.

"Very good, son, thank you." The man made it clear that was all the negotiating he wanted to do.

"I mean it, you old coot. Just give me your money and I'll be on my way. You'll never see me again because I'm leaving this dust hole of a town. Nobody has to get hurt and nobody has to be a hero. I'm thinking you guys must have some high dollar folding money stuffed in those jeans. I'll give you five minutes to produce it, or somebody will remember this day forever." He lifted a bucket from a pile next to him and passed it to Amos as the lead man in the circle. "Don't try anything sneaky as I can see each of you. Any sudden move causes my finger to go back on the trigger."

Amos slowly reached into his pocket and pulled out his wad of bills. "Do you want it all?"

"Of course, do you think I'm stupid enough to come in here to rob you and only take *some* of your money? Give me some credit, Gramps."

Amos dropped his wad of bills into the bucket and passed it left around the circle. The young man swung the gun at the next man for him to speed it up. If he did not see folding money go into the bucket, he'd stand behind the old guy and let him feel the cold gun barrel on his neck until some money came out.

Things went sour when the bucket passed the midpoint of the circle. Everyone saw the movement at the rear of the store, and saw the young man twirl lightning fast and fire one round. There was loud yelp as Ole Jasper, JJ's dog, was thrown back against the wall, definitely hit somewhere. Blood spattered onto the nearest cabinet. Everyone wanted to rush to the dog, but froze to see how the man would react. The only sound was Jasper's soft whine. Everyone knew he was hit, he was hurt, and maybe hurt bad. Meanwhile, Roger had heard the shot from the back room and had enough sense to stay quiet and out of sight.

"I'm sorry, old man. I didn't mean to hit your dog. Ya'll saw how he jumped out like that. He could have been someone in the back of the store trying to surprise me."

"That's just what I've been telling you, son; a loaded gun makes everyone nervous, especially someone like you standing as you are and waving it around. Let's stop this nonsense. Put the gun down so I can tend to Jasper."

"I said I was sorry about your dog, what else do you want from me? Give me that bucket." He snatched the bucket by the handle, a comic figure—if you could see comedy in the situation—with a rusty bucket in one hand and a shiny gun in the other. He backed out the door, jumped into his car, and sped away.

Roger peeked out of the back room holding the juice squeezer, but things were so confused that JJ told him to come back later to pay for it. The police were on the scene within an hour, and Morris, the deputy, interviewed each man individually. After interviewing the regulars, the deputy was so confused by their conflicting stories that he could not put together a coherent police report.

The robbery was fodder for conversation over the next few weeks. The old guys who had been witnesses were in demand as local celebrities, holding court and telling in detail about the day and about their peril. There was bickering about who saw what, who said what, and how much money each man had been forced to put in the bucket, but by this time everyone knew the story and ignored the details that seemed to change daily. People worried about Jasper and everyone commented in typical Southern style, "Ole Jasper's okay, bless his soul. The vet says he'll limp a bit. Luckily the bullet grazed him without hitting bone."

People who came in the store took time to run their fingers through Jasper's fur. To him the ordeal was worth it for the attention. Other than the shot to Jasper, there was no real damage except to the large Pepsi-Cola sign that now had a fresh bullet hole clean through the "o." JJ doubled the price because it was now a valuable artifact.

An APB was broadcast across three counties for the perp who was identified as Curt Penley, a white male, seventeen, heavy build, five foot eight, armed and dangerous. The loot in the bucket was reported in the Marsden Daily News as $65.20. The twenty cents came from poor Billy Varnham who had no folding money but did not want to be shot for holding back, so he dropped in all he had and hoped it didn't rattle.

With no progress catching the perp, everyone tired of hearing the story. Talk of the robbery died down. Marsden was almost back to normal until a Wednesday evening in the third week after the robbery. The boy drove up to the front of the store as JJ was locking up. Curt didn't have a gun and was a lot less nervous. He got out of the car and stood in front of JJ.

"Mr. Junior, can we talk?"

"Of course, son, or should I call you Curt?"

"You can call me Curt. I know you're not happy with me for shooting your dog and for causing all that trouble. The truth is that I don't know what got into me that day. Robbery is stupid, and I must have looked to be one of the dumbest criminals around. I was so nervous. It was a good thing you talked me into holding off the trigger, or I might have hurt someone by accident. Jasper startled me, and I thought someone was coming for me. After the shot, it didn't take much to see that the old dog was not going to shoot me. Is he all right?"

"He's limping but patched up. That was the worst day that ole dog's ever seen."

"Mr. Junior, I've thought a lot about how stupid it was to try to rob you. If I had thought more, I'd have known no one had much money, but I wasn't thinking right. I was depressed after hearing from Annie that she didn't want to see me anymore, and an hour later, I was expelled for a fight the day before. Things are so bad with my mom and dad that the school couldn't even get up with them to tell them about my being expelled. Not that they would have cared; neither of them made it past ninth grade. Without my parents there, the principal called me into his office and gave me the news. I know all of that is no excuse for robbing, but it's the best story I can offer. I'm sorry. Here's all the money I took, maybe you can get it to the right people. I was too addled to recall how far the bucket went around the circle before Jasper jumped out. After we're finished, I'm going to the police to turn myself in. I expect they'll send me to reform camp or something. At least at reform camp there will be place to stay with regular meals and a clean bed. I'm not asking for your understanding. That sorry robbery has been enough of a scare so I'll never try that again."

"Curt, it takes courage to admit you've done something wrong. Thank you for apologizing. From what you say, the robbery was the end of a bad day; one of many bad days you've had lately. It may be the first of a string of bad days to come. Should we call the sheriff from here and save you the drive? Maybe if you stand with me, the police won't think you're a dangerous criminal hiding a firearm and shoot you before they ask questions."

"Thanks, Mr. Junior. Why would you do that for me?"

"I'm not sure, but I have a good feeling about you, Curt. Maybe I had some of the same feelings when I was young."

Time passed and the legal system ran its course. Because it was his first offense, and Marsden was a forgiving town, Curt was put on parole and assigned to community service. The judge allowed him to work off the community service under the guidance of Mr. Julesky Junior. Junior also worked it out that Curt could stay in the small room at the back of his house in return for doing errands and small jobs.

The regular guys continued meeting around the stove at the center of the store while Curt went about his work of cleaning and stocking shelves. A few people spoke to him, but no one brought up the robbery. The men got their money back, including Billy Varnham with his twenty cents.

Curt and Jasper became friends. People who came into the store were surprised at how Jasper followed Curt everywhere rather than sitting in the corner and napping as he'd always done. JJ summed it up for all by explaining that a dog will give you love when you need it most, no matter how down and out you may be.

MISSING HIM

I put fresh tulip petals under the pillows in each bedroom as I'd done when guests were coming. Then I set fire to the house. Even though the fire investigators would never see the tulips, they would certainly find charred leaves in the ashes. I wanted them to think I was gracious.

My husband died two years ago last fall. My most treasured memory is the two of us sitting on the front porch, rocking slowly with the sounds of crickets in the tobacco fields. It seemed a disturbance of nature to whisper even a word to each other and interrupt the cricket song. After forty years of marriage, there was no need to talk—any communication was transmitted through our fingertips. He built our swing with sturdy tobacco shed wood from out back. The swing smelled like drying tobacco, but it was well oiled, and quiet. Melvin liked to just barely rock at a pace that put us both to dozing. That memory sticks with me even though the front porch is empty and the tobacco smell is stale. It's painful to live in a house so infused with memories.

The fire inspector concluded that the fire started in the upstairs bedroom, our bedroom. The sheriff might think I was the one to blame, living there alone as I did, and never going out - maybe some careless act he'd think. If he asked my neighbors as part of the investigation, they would say I lived alone, my mind wandering in the past with my memories. Most people would say I was out of touch; crazy was the harsh word. The fire could look like an accident.

I wasn't supposed to be around to answer questions, but God planned it differently. Unfortunately, I survived the fire. Deputy Tom Norris was the one sent to hear my story. I'd just been released from the hospital and came back to see if I could salvage any valuables. The house was still smoking and there was nothing I could do except look over the smoldering wreckage. I've known Tom and his family all his life. He took me to the station in the front seat of his squad car. He was embarrassed to ask me questions about the fire and said he felt awkward about me sitting in the hard wooden chair beside his desk at the office. He started the interview by assuring me he was just doing his job. He smiled and asked me to let him know if I was feeling weak and we could stop, then he opened by saying that the Sheriff's office was gathering information about the fire, about how it started.

"What happened last night? What do you remember?" he asked.

"Not much. It was a quiet night just like every other night. I talked to my daughter in the afternoon about her children and her husband."

"The inspector says the fire started upstairs in the master bedroom. That's your room isn't it? Where were you when you discovered the fire?"

"I was downstairs and must have dozed off on the couch in front of the TV. Most nights, I settle into the back edge of the couch propped up against the pillow, and within a few minutes, I'm asleep. I often fall asleep there."

"You must sleep soundly. During a fire, there are usually loud noises like crackling and popping from wood burning and the smoke is dense and irritating. In your house, the smoke must have swept down the stairs as the fire spread. It would have been thick after just a short time. You probably got to coughing and that woke you up."

"The stairway is in the back of the house, as far away from the living room as you can get. It could have been some time before any smoke came to the front part of the house, I guess. No windows were open, because I lock them carefully when I watch TV, especially living in the country with no close neighbors. Melvin always made sure I locked and double-checked all the windows before I went to sleep. He preached that you couldn't ever know who might be out there and looking in. With my hearing gone bad, I have to turn up the television. There's never anything going on upstairs, so I probably wasn't listening."

"We don't know what time the fire started, but our best guess is somewhere around 11 o'clock. The fire department didn't get your call until nearly 11:30. Did you call the fire department as soon as you knew the house was on fire?"

"I guess. I was in a daze - shocked and paralyzed all at once. I went from surprise at how there could be so much smoke to snippets of thought on what that meant and then thoughts on what I could save. My daughter got me a cell phone for emergencies and it must have been in the pocket of my robe. It took me some time to remember the phone and to make the call. On the front lawn, I could see the smoke and flames coming from the upstairs, but I never suspected how far the fire had spread. You're right, I do sleep soundly, but I must have just awakened in the middle of a dream or something; my mind was slow to understand how serious it was. Even now, I wouldn't believe such a terrible thing had happened if the smoking house wasn't there as evidence."

"Memories of my whole life were in that house. I wouldn't know where to start to carry out things to save, and all the smoke and my coughing were too much for me to find anything in the house anyway. Isn't the first instinct to save yourself?

I knew I was the only one in the house. I don't have pets, so I saved myself by stumbling out the front door through a cloud of smoke. I watched the place go up in flames from the front yard."

"Do you remember any of your neighbors talking to you? Witnesses say they came to your house after seeing the smoke and flames. Several of them saw you come out the front door, coughing, eyes closed from the smoke, your robe flying behind you in the wind. Even though they asked you if there was anyone or anything in the house that needed to be saved, you just looked at them, eyes glassy and watering, and didn't say anything. They said you were staring straight ahead, shaking your head between coughs. Do you remember any of that?"

"Of course I remember the neighbors. I'm not that feeble yet, but I never heard them talking to me. I guess they were there when I came out of the house, but I can't remember who was there or what they said."

"Now comes the hard part for me to ask. The fire inspector found rags under the beds upstairs, rags soaked in gasoline. That's why he said the fire started in the bedroom. It's surprising what an expert can tell, even though everything around is burned to ashes. He seems to think that the gasoline smell should have been obvious to anyone in the house, even someone downstairs. Did anyone visit you that day, anyone who might have gone upstairs?"

"No. I've been alone for days and just talked to my daughter in Cleveland that afternoon, but no one visited."

"Blanche, how do you think the rags and the gasoline got up to the bedrooms?" The deputy seemed perplexed. "There were worn electric plugs in that room and the inspector said that any one of them could have had a break in the wiring to produce a spark. With all those gas fumes in the room, it wouldn't take long for the whole place to go up. Do any memories come back as we're talking?"

"No, honestly all I remember is having dinner that night; some leftover soup I heated up on the stove. I walked out to the front porch to do a safety check and then settled in front of the television and fell asleep. That's all I remember until the smoke, the coughing, and running out the front door. I wish my memory were better and I could help you more, but that's all I remember."

"I hate to say this, Blanche, but the sheriff thinks you may know more than you're telling us. Since there's nobody else to ask, your memory is the most important thing in investigating this fire. Questions always come up in fires like this; questions about how people sometimes start a fire to get insurance money. I don't know anything about your finances or how much Melvin left you, but I'll tell you that we have to investigate all the possibilities. It seems like we're prying into people's private business, but that fire was a big one, destroying the house and everything in it. If there's an insurance policy, we'll find out."

"Melvin handled all those financial things while he was alive. I think he had insurance on the place, but in the two years since he died, I haven't paid a dime to an insurance company. I guess that means they canceled the policy. All my things were in there and now there might be no insurance. What will I do?" "Blanche, this community takes care of its own. People are working on things for you.

Let me ask this another way and see if you might remember better. Is it possible that you could have been upstairs that afternoon cleaning and dusting with some cleaning products that might burn easily, some gasoline even, and forgot the rags under the beds?"

"I'm a tidy housekeeper, always have been, and I believe in dusting and mopping, but I don't believe in using any special cleaning products. Besides, the furniture up there is clean and dust is the only thing that accumulates. Now, I've told you I don't remember much about that night.

I know people say that my memory has slipped, but I can only tell you what I remember, and the last thing I remember is that I fell asleep in front of the television and woke up from a sound sleep coughing from the smoke all around me."

"Well, whatever happened, you're lucky to be alive. If you had been more of a sound sleeper, I think it might have been too late for you to overcome the smoke and get out alive. People in town are getting together some things to help you out during this difficult time. They are coming over to talk to you and help figure out what you're going to do for meals and a bed to sleep in. We've been in contact with your daughter, and she's on her way back to town. Yes ma'am, you're lucky to be alive."

"I guess I am lucky to be alive."

I stewed as I sat outside Tommy Norris' office. No one had gotten there yet to tell me what the future would be and who I'd be spending it with, beholden for everything. My biggest worry was how to avoid one of those Care Homes. My daughter might come and she would spend some time showing a caring face, then she'd head back to her fancy house in Cleveland.

Damn, I can't seem to do anything right. If Melvin were here, he would have known how to do a better job and I wouldn't be in this tight spot. Just five minutes more—I'm sure of it—would have finished things. He gave me the idea when I visited him last week. We talk every day, and talking is as easy as sitting together on the front porch those many years ago. He understood when I cried about being lonely in that house and about missing him so. His voice came through as if he were standing beside me, a soft whisper in my head.

"Take the gas can in the garage, soak a few rags or just any clothes from the dresser and put them under all the beds upstairs. Give one of the electrical cords a good twist, but be careful not to shock yourself. Then drop the cord on the carpet, and that's all it will take.

Go downstairs and wait. Follow your normal routine and then rest on the couch in front of the TV. To make it look good, call our daughter in case they investigate any calls, and just give her some light chatter. You'll fall asleep quick enough and the next thing you know we'll be together."

The fire had worked exactly as he said it would, except for my part. I wasn't supposed to wake up with smoke burning my lungs, coughing so hard I almost peed my pants. Even though I'd taken one of his sleeping pills, it wasn't enough. Now I'm here with the sheriff breathing down my neck about an insurance fire and there is no money, no house, and I'm still missing Melvin. Tommy said I was lucky. I don't consider it lucky at all.

Melvin and I joked about our dying. We wanted it to be a clean job; we both would go together in an accident and our daughter could deal with the aftermath. Even though we travelled light with as few tangible goods as possible, we still had a bunch of stuff. After Melvin died, I did my best to get rid of most of it, but you need a few things to live, even to live a basic life. Melvin came up with the idea of burning the house and getting rid of everything in one giant pyre and that would finish things like we'd intended. If the plan had worked, I would've joined him last night and we'd be together forever. Now only half of the plan is done; I'm still here, but nothing else is.

Maybe I can drive the car over a cliff, maybe that spot about fifteen miles outside of town on the road to Jacksonville where the guardrail is torn out. Going over the cliff will not hurt anybody and people will put it down to a heart attack or stroke. Maybe when I visit him this afternoon, Melvin will approve. If not, I know he'll have another plan. He's always been good at solving problems.

I'll ask Tommy to drive me to the house to get the car. Let me find the keys in my purse, and maybe we can get it done tonight just after it gets dark.

Damn I miss him.

RAT-A-TAT-TAT

I needed money, and I needed it fast. My debt was due, and the impending visit from Mr. Hairy and Mr. Ugly made the urgency clear. Their message would be that Rudy was an understanding guy, but Rudy's patience had a limit. In the beginning, before I got the money, he and I were the best of friends. We talked about old times over burgers and beer and had a laugh about enjoying the luxuries of life. I shared that I'd needed some extra money for any of those luxuries after getting out of state prison. To help me through this tough time, Rudy volunteered to loan me three thousand dollars. His weekly rate of eighteen percent interest was a bargain in the industry and it was so much of a bargain that he asked me not to broadcast the details. The loan was a special favor because we were friends. Rudy's associate slid a printed loan agreement across the table, and after I signed, the associate passed the cash over in a neat package tied with kitchen twine. With this kind of loan, written agreements are fluff, so I didn't read it. The implied contract was simple: if the loanee didn't pay the principal plus interest on time, one of Rudy's associates, Hairy or Ugly, would find the guy and offer a reminder.

Before meeting Rudy and his three thousand, I'd kept my head above water with whatever low paying jobs I could find as an ex-con. What little money I earned went for a single room and personal items. The food was free at the soup kitchen and occasionally even palatable, but there were no luxuries.

Rudy's money lasted me less than two weeks. I loved the horses, and when I had money, the track pulled me like a magnet. Gamblers knew there were up and down cycles, and although the cycles were mostly unexplainable, performing a ritual helped winning. My most successful ritual was to order a Bloody Mary before I placed a bet and drink it down in gulps after I placed the bet. I'd studied the rituals of other gamblers: clapping and turning around twice seemed to work sometimes, as did hopping on one leg or walking backwards through the ticket stiles. Any regular track patron appreciated unusual behavior as some kind of ritual. When I was losing, I believed there were no lucky charms in gambling and everything was chance…or maybe I just hadn't found the right one yet, but when I was winning…

At the track that sunny morning, I ordered a Bloody Mary and placed all of Rudy's money on a nag called Rat-a-Tat-Tat to win. It was a hunch because with that name there had to be some luck in the horse. After leaving the window and gulping the drink, I remembered that the three grand was only a loan. Seven minutes later, when another horse crossed the line, I was alone, minus the three grand, amid the chits littering the floor and without my betting friends. The track could take money just that quickly in the time between the opening gate and the leader passing the pole.

Over the years, I'd won more than fifty thousand clear when I was on a winning streak. My weakness was that I never recognized that winning was least likely during a losing streak. Usually I kept betting until the winnings were gone, confident a win would come with the next bet. Foolish optimism convinced me all would be well.

As I stood outside the turnstiles with nothing to bet and a little over four thousand to pay off in forty-eight hours, the Bloody Mary refluxed back to me along with an idea. I still had a kind of retirement fund, the insurance on my ex-wife's house, and if I could somehow collect it, my troubles might be over. The insurance payoff would be enough to pay off Rudy's loan. If I could convince him the money was coming, he might hold off his guys. My off-the-cuff plan was that by some chance event, the house might burn, and after a short time, I'd receive a check for the insurance. Rudy was a patient man and might accept the plan if he saw a copy of the policy. He was also a businessman and knew that interest and late fees would increase profit. If I could assure him that the house would catch fire within a few days, he might believe me, and my right pinky finger would remain attached.

Charleen, my ex, hated when I drove up in a noisy cloud of dust. I was her first and third husband, and my visits had been a saga of hardship and misfortune for her. That was just the way I was. She knew whatever tale I told her would end with my asking for cash.

"Hey Babe. You look great for a hot afternoon; there's a glow about you. You've improved considerably since the divorce. Have you missed me?"

"No, I haven't missed you. Does a dog miss fleas—both are irritations, but your irritation lasts a lot longer."

"Is that any way to talk to someone you've walked down the aisle with twice? You sound like you still hold a grudge."

"There's no accounting for my poor judgment the first time, but the second time was just God-awful stupid. As for grudges, we both know the answer all too well." I held back on the rest of my thoughts, he's a show off, just a big show off. It took me three years of marriage to find that out and yet I stayed for another five.

"Charleen, what do you say about a little afternoon delight? Bet you haven't lost any of your moves. You look like you've been taking care of yourself. When we're basking in the afterglow, I have a deal to tell you about, a deal with easy money."

"Free sex is what you usually want, but what do you really want, you no-good piece of shit?"

"I hate to spoil the surprise, but the deal involves making money without having to do anything. Easiest money you've made since you took to lying on your back for a living."

"Another half-baked plan I'll bet. Sweat it out here on the porch and let me change into something presentable. As long as there's no sex involved, I like the sound of easy money without doing work."

I told her the plan and explained her share of the money—twenty thousand of the one hundred thousand insurance payout. Although she complained about the split, she'd never find twenty thousand on the street. Her work would be minimal, and more importantly, her risk was low. If things went sour, it would be my problem; I'd take the fall, and she would be an innocent bystander. I dropped the hint that if I screwed up, the insurance company might award her all the money. The glint in her eyes told me that the plan intrigued her. Reluctantly, she agreed, but I knew her well enough to know she didn't want to appear too willing. She would need to clear out some of her stuff from the house and stay with her sister for a few nights. Some of her stuff needed to be inside or it would look suspicious. I replayed the scheme, and once she'd bought in, I mentally set the date and fleshed out the plan.

I met with Rudy and his associate, Elrod, the next day. Rudy's disposition improved considerably at the mention of insurance. I showed him the policy with the payout page clipped. He liked the plan and told Elrod to get some donuts for us to seal the deal.

Rudy summed it up well. "If you can pull this off, kid, we'll be square. If you pull it off flawlessly, I may be able to find a position for you in my organization. That kind of regular employment will improve your long-term prospects. Just to be sure the plan moves along as we anticipate, Elrod here will be going with you."

Rudy explained that burning down houses was an essential skill his associates needed to learn. For Elrod, burning this one, his first, would mean a step up in the organization, a kind of career advancement. Rudy always encouraged his employees to expand their horizons. This type of work required a flexible schedule and skills not learned in trade schools, so on-the-job training was the best way to learn quality work. Rudy explained his career advancement plan, and we all nodded, toasted with a jelly donut, and agreed on the date for the following Friday. As a goodwill gesture, he suspended the accrual of interest for a week and left Elrod and I to work out the details of the caper. Rudy took the donuts.

Elrod and I drove by the house to survey the neighborhood. We agreed to make a second trip that night to see how things looked after the neighbors went to bed. On the trip back, we confirmed that the neighborhood was quiet, that no one walked their dog after eleven, and that lights were out everywhere by midnight. I thought gasoline would be the most reliable flammable and assigned Elrod to bring a full can. My plan was to drop by my motel room to get a few old shirts and underwear as combustibles and meet Elrod downtown at one thirty Friday morning.

"Wear black, Elrod." As if it needed to be said. In our short time together, I suspected Elrod might be a little slow, so it was better to spell everything out to avoid costly mistakes. We only had the one chance, and if we blew it, I would need to get out of town fast. If Elrod was stupid enough to twist an ankle, break a leg, or suffer some other unexpected tragedy, he was on his own. Those were the breaks in this business. I laughed at the pun and picked out lightweight, high-topped support shoes, my lucky shoes from the track.

With no money, there was little for me to do from Wednesday to Friday except watch a lot of television in the motel room and spend time with some of my buddies at the soup kitchen. It was best that Charleen and I did not talk.

Early Friday morning, I sat in the front seat of Elrod's car next to the gas can and torn undergarments. My black turtleneck matched Elrod's black t-shirt, and we both had stocking caps and black shoe polish to cover our faces, the image of commandos on a risky night mission.

We banditos parked the car a block away and hurried across dark yards in shadows. I knew the layout of the neighborhood, and after we got to Charleen's backyard, I broke a window and went through the back door. It didn't take long to open the laundry room door and drop half the rags, douse them with gasoline, and close the door. Speed was important. I sent Elrod upstairs to stuff some rags under the bathroom sink and soak them with liberal pours of gasoline.

Our plan went sour when Elrod pulled a match and struck it before he left the bathroom. The combination of fumes and spilled gas blew the door off the bathroom. When I heard the explosion, I knew exactly what Elrod had done. My suspicion was confirmed by a flaming Elrod screaming as he ran down the stairs. It did not take me long to put together Plan B, and Elrod was nowhere in the plan. As a frantic burning Elrod ran past me, I gave him enough of a tap on the head with a convenient iron pipe that he stopped screaming. He continued burning as his trail of flame headed for the laundry room rags. I stepped out the back door, relocked it, and checked through the window to be sure Elrod continued to be the flaming asshole he'd always been. I chuckled again at the pun and headed for the car.

It was bad luck that Elrod had driven, because the keys were still in his front pocket, but I knew the neighborhood well enough to walk the several blocks up the street. No one had heard the screams or seen the smoke, yet. I'd be long gone before I heard any sirens. The house burned nicely.

I couldn't have planned it better. Elrod was the perfect foil, and his car cinched it. Rudy would not like that Elrod was gone, but it was his own fault, lighting the match too early, and Rudy would understand. Who could be that stupid? I texted Charleen that things were happening as expected and settled into my motel room to await the next step. As I eased into bed, my hand slipped under the pillow, and I had a religious experience. God had pinned a one-hundred-dollar bill to the inside of the pillow. My only explanation was that the money was God's way of encouraging me to head to the track for the first race on Saturday.

This time there would be no rituals, no Bloody Mary, nor any peculiar body movements to ensure success. I walked directly to the window, eyes straight ahead, and placed the hundred on a horse named Scooby Doo to win at 50:1 odds. Those were long, almost impossible odds. The bookies must have thought that nag could not even finish, let alone win, but the bet felt more right than ever before. I didn't need to look at the board or listen to the broadcast. I just hung around the window, knowing I'd collect. After the results were announced, I had a wad of just over five thousand in twenties. I set four thousand aside to cover debts, went back to the window with one thousand, and placed in all on Rusty Nail to win. That bet had the same feeling of being right. Another three thousand came in. As I pocketed the wad of folded money, I sensed that my lucky streak was over. To my credit, I listened to that little man inside who told me to walk away. I left, my pockets stuffed with fresh twenties and a new outlook on life.

On the walk home, I peeled off Rudy's share from the cash plus two thousand I'd give Charleen until the insurance was settled. If I stiffed her, she would be at the police station within the day to tell the whole story. After covering everything, I was still about three grand in the clear, a damn good day of work. Prospects were looking up. With Elrod gone, Rudy would surely find a spot for me. That would increase my stock with Rudy and get me a regular job, maybe a job with health benefits. In addition, there was a better than average chance the insurance company would pay Charleen after they found Elrod. Finally, I had cash in my pocket, enough for walking-around money and for pinning that lucky hundred back under my pillow.

At the corner, I turned right towards Charleen's sister's house. With the two thousand up front, she'd find a way to show her gratitude. I bet she'd suppressed some sexual fantasies that needed release. Who knew, she might be so enthralled after the roll to give marriage number three a try. After all, it was my lucky day.

THE NEXT TIME

Patsy liked to think of it as her hot fudge sundae smile— inviting, warm, and sweet. She practiced smiling in front of her bathroom mirror until she'd perfected the look, a playful balance between a young girl's innocence and her hidden sensuality. She could deliver the smile effortlessly, and coupled with a sway to her hips, it implied a promise of adventure. She always got a response.

Ever since his first breakfast at the diner two weeks ago, Patsy marked Glen as a person of interest. He looked to be in his early forties with gray eyes, swept back dark hair, and the hint of a once-great body under his flannel shirt. His easy smile showed plenty of straight white teeth—the look of an unusual and provocative character. Patsy was used to two kinds of customers at the diner: men with potbellies who hoped to score attention with young waitresses and women with pot bellies, makeup troweled on, who came to catch up on gossip.

Glen sat at the far end of the counter, and she had to walk the distance under his stare. He scanned her body from her feet to her hair and paused at the interesting spots. It wasn't a creepy stare, but more appreciative. She secretly hoped he scanned her body again as she walked away and that he continued to be interested. After the first day, he didn't need a menu. His order was the same: scrambled eggs, wet; patty sausage; grits; white toast, heavy on the butter; and coffee, hot, with the cup filled often.

After the first week, they became casually friendly—casually because mornings were busy. People who sat at the counter liked their food hot and fast without chat. Seats turned over quickly as folks ate and got the hell out in a hurry to get to work. She was aware that he'd noticed her, and toward the end of the week, she slowed service to the counter customers after the first rush to spend a little extra time with him. He appreciated the attention and tipped a few dollars, a big tip for breakfast at a Marsden diner. They moved on to first names after that week. He had a North Carolina accent, not one from around Marsden, but maybe from somewhere south like New Bern or Wilmington. Patsy lived in Marsden all of her twenty years and had never seen him before—she would've remembered.

She'd had suitors in Marsden, local boys who treated a girl kindly on the way to bed. Their attention and spending dwindled while they looked for their next target. Patsy was tired of the bed swap and wanted something more tangible, something she could build into a future. Twenty years old was prime time for Marsden girls who wanted to settle down. After her last bitter breakup, she set her sights on older men, working through dates with the thirty-to-fifty crowd. She listened to their wining about wives or old girlfriends, but they spent too little money and there was no future in it. The few promising dates wanted to hang around dark corners in a bar, away from the public, as if they were undercover CIA agents.

Since that first day, she sensed Glen was different. From his generous tips, she could tell that he had a few dollars more than the local boys had. He was in town for a few weeks investigating two suspicious arson cases. In a small town like Marsden, everyone knew details of the cases and had their own opinion of who had done what, but Glen was the expert hired by the insurance company to give an authoritative report.

By the second week, he started coming in for lunch, taking the same seat and ordering the house special cheeseburger, well done, with lettuce, tomato, onion, and fries on the side. The burger had to be well done because he didn't like burger juice dripping down his shirt. He liked a large fountain cherry Pepsi with plenty of crushed ice and sipped it direct from the glass. Patsy took that as a sign of a real man. She watched his lips on the edge of the glass as he took deep swallows. When the glass was empty, he chewed on the ice chips and looked in her direction with each crunch. She felt his look run through her as if she'd dipped her fingertips in a bucket of ice, and he knew it. She wanted more but hadn't spoken about it yet. She needed to give him a hint... and a woman knows how to give a hint. On Friday of that second week, he asked her out and was surprisingly shy about it because of their age difference.

He took her to the fancy steakhouse on the way to Kinston, and the evening went well. She looked good in a conservative outfit that hugged her body without being obvious. They connected with an easy conversation style; he asked about her work and whether she'd been to college.

"No, no college. My parents told me we couldn't afford it even if I lived at home. I needed a job, so I started working at the diner. I've been there since, two years ago. It's been hard to save much on this salary, but I was a good student in high school and hope to get some help with a scholarship to go to community college next semester."

"I suspected you were a practical girl working her way through college, maybe majoring in something in the medical field. Funny how first impressions form, especially with no real facts. You probably don't have any idea what you want to study, but I thought it might be in some medical field." He smiled and looked down as if laughing at his impressions of her.

"You're right on; I want to study medical coding because I can work from home on a flexible schedule and still work at the diner." She asked about his work and he gave her a high-level summary. "I work for an insurance company and investigate house fires. The company needs to know as much as they can about what might have caused the fire." She sensed that in his work life, he kept information private, and even though she was curious, she did not pry.

"How can you find any clues in a burned-out building," she asked. She looked at his clothes and they both laughed about the lingering smell of smoke on his clothes. "I'm sorry, I didn't mean that your clothes smelled." He smiled at her embarrassment.

"I don't smell the smoke after all this time; it's part of the job. I hang my work clothes in the closet and the smoke migrates to everything else. I have to throw things out that I've barely worn because the laundry lady can't get rid of the smell. It's OK to wear smoky clothes to work, but I start to run out of good clothes after about a week."

He suggested they go to a movie nearby, and she agreed. He gave her the choice of a romantic comedy or an action shoot'em up and was not surprised with her choice. The movie was a sappy romance, and she cried. He offered a smoky handkerchief and took her hand. Both liked the contact and continued it after the movie. She wasn't hungry, so he took her home.

At her door, he was shy. "I had a great time tonight, thank you. Maybe we can go out again, hopefully next weekend. My work is nearly done in the cases here, and I'll be leaving in a few weeks." She knew what that meant and respected him for not starting anything serious during his remaining time in Marsden. At the door, he looked like he wanted to kiss her, but did not. She'd had enough dodging, took his hand, and pulled him into her darkened hallway.

"I need to see what kind of kisser you are. I've been thinking about it all night. Do you think I'm a bad person? You probably know that all girls want to know how a guy kisses." Her comment seemed as sappy as the movie. Gentle hands moved with intertwined fingers, holding and releasing, his arms around her waist and hers around his neck. He kissed her softly, gauging her reaction, and then accelerated the kiss, each playing off each other. Pulling apart and re-engaging, kissing deeper and harder as time passed slowly. He pulled away and looked into her eyes, asking for direction. Her eyes replied...yes. He nodded, acknowledging the invitation, and smiled.

"I know I'll regret this decision all the way home, but I want to know you better before we get involved. Can we delay until next time?" They pressed together for the last few minutes.

"I'll be working down the road in Kinston after this job is finished. My territory is Eastern North Carolina, so I'm never too far away. I hope you'll meet me when you can. She smiled her hot fudge sundae smile and kissed him lightly as she closed the door.

Behind the door, her smile continued with hope for the next time.

THE DOCTOR IN TOWN

Fate, the mother of us all, guided me here in 1957. I drove a dusty 1950 Powerglide Chevy into town looking for a job. Cars parked at angles studded the four blocks of Main Street, and busy citizens crowded both sides of the street. There was a small vacant brick two-story building at the north end of town, a block beyond the established stores. Negotiations were quick. The owner needed a tenant, and the combination first floor office and second floor apartment were suitable for a businessman who didn't mind being on the edge of town. That was not a problem for my business. It took a day to find a sign maker and hang my shingle above the door. Carl Jordan, M.D. was open for business. I was the only doctor in town, so business picked up nicely.

In the late 1950s, the title of general practitioner meant something. People always got sick, and in that first year, I established trust by providing competent care and by being available for emergencies. I took care of any patient, black or white, rich or poor, ornery or not, and I made house calls. If a drunk wandered in, the nurse sent him away, and he came back when he was sober. My office hours were eight to five, five days a week, but that was only a guideline. If a patient knocked after hours, I yelled out the upstairs window for them to sit on the porch, and I'd be down shortly.

I remembered the names of most patients because they were my neighbors, and I saw a variety of diseases and stayed with some to comfort them as they died. In the office, the interview with the patient was the most important part of the encounter. People needed to tell their story in their own terms and I learned to listen and smile as they talked. In those early days, my hands were my greatest asset, warm, smooth, and neatly groomed. Someone told me that people didn't trust a doctor with dirty hands and so I washed my hands after coming into the room so the patients knew they were clean. In the beginning, it was difficult for me to examine patients because I disliked physical contact, but when people complimented my gentle touch, I became more comfortable.

Examining a patient was like playing a fine instrument, my warm gentle touch started well away from the tender area and slowly worked toward their particular pone. During the exam, I nodded often to encourage patients to add details to their story. If someone complained of pain in their chest, I'd gently palpate the back and front, feeling for tender spots. If I found tenderness, it was the end of my search and I knew what to do; if not, I'd listen with my scope and decide on something different. If their chest rattled, they went home with pills dispensed by the nurse from our back office supply; if their chest was quiet, they went home with the same pills, but a different color. The results were the same—patients most often got better. All my pills looked similar, large, or medium sized and colored blue, white, or bright yellow. It was easy to buy colored double 0 wax capsules out of town and fill them with sugar. Placebo pills were common at the time, and the nurse always instructed patients to swallow them whole and not chew them, so they never tasted the sugar. I used simple medicines because they worked.

The mechanics of laboratory testing did not interest me, only the mystery and manifestations of disease. Refinement of my medical knowledge came from trial and error. On a back office shelf was my single reference, the Merck Manual. I consulted it when I had a difficult case, and the pages became worn over the years. In most cases, the manual proved adequate. Those were the times of the worst cases of polio, widespread tuberculosis, and all the childhood illnesses. I saw all those diseases. Vaccination of children was not common.

Payment for my services was a challenge. Few people had readily available cash, so most offered trades or asked for credit until their crops came in. I collected food, farm animals, and canned preserves and patients saved their best stuff for the doctor. If I took care of all three kids in a family for their colds, I might get a smoked ham; if a farmer's wife had the vapors, the husband brought a few thick steaks. When I had enough food, I took handmade clothing.

As with most general practitioners, people came with common ailments: colds, scrapes, and fever. Emergencies and house calls were always in the middle of the night for patients too sick to leave their bed. An emergency for a farmer had the same importance whether it was a cow in labor or his wife's spells. In both cases, I prescribed the same sugar pills, and more often than not, the wife and the cow got better. I saw joy, grief, and the loss of life, often in the same week.

Common diseases tended to improve in a day or two, and if not, I sent the patient on to a specialist in Wilmington. Children were the biggest challenges because what looked like a cold might actually be a serious disease like polio or meningitis and would require immediate treatment. The city doctors appreciated the prompt referral and always let me know how things turned out.

Toward the end of a long day, I sometimes failed in my care. The best I could do was to imagine the person in front of me as a skeleton stripped of skin. I was able to follow the thread of their history but I saw only a talking group of bones. Often I asked them to come back in the morning for a fresh look. People saw my foibles and accepted me.

Most days I was able to puzzle out a patient's problem using common sense. My treatments reinforced the placebo principle— examine carefully, treat with confidence, and expect a cure. Surprisingly, confidence was the most important component. Confidence was an effective medicine because if a patient believed I knew how to treat their problem, their belief was enough; patients tried to get better because it was expected. When people heard my diagnosis, they believed me, and symptoms that were unbearable before the visit, with my reassurance, became bearable. I had a nervous tic, rubbing my knuckles back and forth across my lips and teeth as I thought about a difficult case. The tic initially gave patients a start, but then eventually instilled confidence in my diagnostic skills. The tic helped solve a surprising number of vexing problems.

I learned that it was important to observe all the clues in the encounter. I remember a wife who was nervous waiting for my diagnosis of her husband's illness. She softly rubbed her trembling finger across the hair of her eyebrow and then repeated the motion on the other eyebrow. She sat silently beside her husband, looking between us. To hide his embarrassment, he looked straight ahead at the sunset print on the wall, studying the print and the color of the sunset. He was used to facing the sun in tobacco fields, his face was lined with crow's feet, and his right foot tapped, tapped on the floor to some rhythm in his head. She looked cautiously at her husband and then back to me, willing him to talk about his symptoms, to be truthful about his weight loss, lack of appetite, and the pains in his stomach. He was most often silent, not ready, so she told the story. I watched her hands and her eyes for clues as to what she needed. It was obvious that he had a cancer of some kind, likely terminal. Before I said the words, she knew her suspicions were true, and her eyes asked what could be done. She wanted my guidance on the path from here to there, but he never spoke. Diagnosing cancer was terrible, but not difficult. Someone with a wasting disease, steady pain, and jaundice had the bad disease. Finding where the cancer was located was not important back then. People did not want to know the type; they just accepted that it was cancer, an untreatable condition in their mind. Every day they stayed above ground was a blessing, a day to be used to work as long as they were able.

One morning, a car weaving down Main Street hit a man, and the patrons of the Mecca grill had an excellent view of the accident. I was sitting at a table in the front window, looked out at the splattered man, and then resumed my breakfast, knowing the man was already dead and beyond my services. None of the patrons questioned my decision.

Through weeks, then years, I learned to appreciate the strength of the human body—the oldest to the youngest bodies—and how they adapted as they aged. It was common to see an old granny and then a newborn baby, one after the other in a morning, and the diversity of life amazed me.

There were many times when I went to a person's home, often in the middle of the night. On one visit, the spouse opened the front door, nodded, and led me upstairs to their bedroom. It was a clean room infused with the smell of sickness. On the wall opposite the window, there was a huge poster bed with a white lace canopy. The patient, a man I had seen only rarely, was propped up in the bed, leaning against large feather pillows, his breathing so labored that he could barely get more than a few words out without pausing. There was an odor of urine from the bed and damp washed sheets hung out the window to dry. By way of decoration in the room, hanging on a nail in the middle of the wall was a crayon drawing of a man. Underneath the drawing in a child's handwriting was: To Dear Papa. This man was Papa.

Another woman told me about her husband: "That man is disturbed, sick you know. He's never been all there, what with staring into space rather than looking me in the eye like a normal person, talking crazy sentences about the devil or someone following him or trying to poison him. He never tells normal things anymore, and people stay well away from him. I've never known for him to hurt anybody, but with crazy people, you never know when they're just going to snap and go for your throat."

She went on in that vein for some time, and I found that letting her get it out was the best tonic, looking at her face and listening with my hands crossed in my lap. Eventually, her tape ran out and she went back into herself. Our conversation continued, but she avoided my eyes to look down at my hands, as if they would give the diagnosis.

Then, one week, my routine changed. Odd feelings stirred in me, and I felt something alive moving deep inside my abdomen, tightening and squeezing, not yet pain but becoming pain. The feeling became worse and changed to pain. I had examined enough patients to know the diagnosis. My nurse and I decided to close the office gradually over the next three months.

At home, I turned to thoughts of God and an afterlife. I became philosophical about the extremes of life, knowing that the boundary between life and death could be measured like the narrow path of a tornado, and like the tornado, disease was unstoppable. With each day, the boundary moved closer, making me wonder about the next adventure. My ego believed that medicine could hold back that boundary, and that my will could determine the path for it to miss me.

A week after the office closed, I sat in the sun on the front porch and looked at my hands. I was surprised at how bony they had become, the flesh now stripped away. The knuckles were prominent, and the skin was stretched tight around every joint, yet my grip was strong and my gentle touch was the same touch that so many patients recalled.

I had seen life end in suddenness, a merciful transition between living and then not, and I had seen the opposite—a slow, often painful process of ending that fostered replaying, regret, and only a few pleasant memories. Which path would I prefer if it were in my power? My preference didn't matter because the choice was made for me.

I hoped my legacy would live on, but I doubted it. After I'd gone, people would forget the good and only remember the bad. My greatest secret would go with me into the grave. On my scout into town in 1957, I was looking for easy money, but instead found my destiny on a path that was irreversible. In the end, if people thought I was a doctor and helped them, then I was their doctor.

THE CAT HOUSE

There were seventeen cats living in my house. Only gradually did I recognize that seventeen was too many, but stray cats were my obsession. For years, I'd rescued stray cats on the drive between my job and home, but eventually, I drove on, apologizing to any cats I saw beside the road. Initially the rescued cats lived in the basement, but they seemed discontented and collected at the door, so I let them upstairs. Within a week, they had divided the house into territories.

I spent considerable time and money meeting their needs: the right food, individual feeding schedules, the right litter smell, and so many other customizations. The cost of keeping the cats took most of my paycheck so that I couldn't afford a night out with a date or a lunch with friends. Just last week I learned that their favorite canned food had been replaced with a more expensive brand. Something had to give.

As a cost-saving measure, I vowed to get rid of fifteen cats before the end of the month. Which cats would have to go would be a hard decision, but my reasoning was that the cats were strays that had lived a pampered life. I dreaded taking the unlucky ones to the shelter—everyone knows what happens to shelter cats—but the shelter was better than turning them out onto the street. At the shelter, there was at least a chance of adoption. For days I watched each cat, mentally choosing the ones to go and the ones to stay. I think they suspected a change was coming and acted peevish with me.

I didn't know it, but on the second Friday in April, the cats started planning an escape. Escape talk started as hushed whispers among the most discontented cats. Like a planned prison break where every inmate knew the generalities, only the active planners knew the specifics. I learned about the plan from Sophie, a puffy Turkish Van and the senior cat. In their meeting, she spoke against an escape because of the loss of stability—a warm bed, premium food, and a clean litter box. She gave me her estimate that six of the seventeen would not leave, six were neutral, and the remaining five wanted freedom. In their planning meeting the day before, she reported that Buster, a majestic Russian Blue and the natural leader of the escape group, had outlined the considerable hurdles. A coordinated effort by six cats would be impossible without meticulous planning; doors had to be opened and an escape route mapped out.

Sophie reported that in the meeting the giddy younger cats strayed off point to describe what they would pack in their travel bags— favorite toys and dry food. Buster brought them back to reality by pointing out that without fingers to pack a bag, carrying anything was hopeless. He said such frivolous talk was a waste of time, like talking about a fish driving a car. To lighten the tension, Rainbow, second in command, told a dream he'd had about a tabby cat walking in the shadows with a red saddlebag over his back. Everyone laughed at the inside joke because everyone knew that cats hated the color red.

Sophie's inside knowledge gave me the specifics of the plan, but not the reasons. Buster was my favorite and the most sophisticated and it hurt that he wanted to leave. He had always been aloof with me, arrogant even. I wanted to know specific information and corralled him by his feed bowl. I held his head so that he had to look at me and started, "Sophie told me that you want to leave with some of the other cats. Will you talk to me about it?" No answer from Buster. He wriggled out of my grasp and scooted away.

According to Sophie, after my encounter with Buster, the team was nervous about being discovered and changed the date for the escape to before dawn in two days. I started to make my own plans and thought that everything could work out if I left the door ajar to let them leave. With six gone, I'd have to take only a few to the shelter. On the evening before the escape, I left the door open…

That's the last thing I remember. When I opened my eyes, I was in a bed in an unfamiliar room with soft white lights and dull gray walls. My wrists were strapped to a bed rail. I knew the cats could not have managed to get me into a bed and restrain my wrists. I tried moving my fingers, but a dark curtain slid over my eyes. After an indeterminate time, I awoke sitting in a chair. Bright morning sunshine was streaming through a nearby window. Where were the cats? Hazy thoughts drifted in and out and I found it pleasurable to hum softly.

After some time, a man entered the room. He was dressed in a gray suit, natty vest, and shiny black wingtip shoes. Everything about him was crisp and clean. His close-cropped beard was flecked with gray, the same tone of gray as his suit. He sat across from me in a straight-backed wooden chair, crossed his legs, and spoke.

"Well now, how are we feeling this morning?" His tenor voice had a condescending tone reserved for the mentally challenged, drunks, or young children.

I was surprised to hear my voice answer from a distant place. "I slept well, I think. Where am I?"

"You're being taken care of, no worries there. We've got everything under control, and you're safe."

"Safe? Was I in danger?"

"It depends on what you consider danger. There is no danger from anyone except yourself; no one is trying to hurt you, and no one is following you. You can relax. We're here to help you." He stretched each syllable out, and a weak smile played across his face.

"I never felt that I was in danger. The last thing I remember is being at home feeding my cats, and getting ready for dinner. I'd planned to help Buster and five other cats escape so I wouldn't have to take so many cats to the shelter. I don't remember anything after that. What day is this?"

"This is Thursday. To help you orient, the name of the day is written on that white board across the room."

"Thursday? It can't be. I just finished a meeting at work on Monday. Where did the rest of the days go?"

"You've been asleep since Monday night when you came in."

"In? Where is in?"

"The hospital, that's where you are. Not the medical kind of hospital, although we do have some patients who need medical care. This is a psychiatric hospital."

"I don't believe you. What happened to me that I would possibly need to be in a psychiatric hospital?"

"You had a breakdown, technically a break with reality that profoundly affected your ability to care for yourself. Your neighbors found you wandering in the street outside your house, mumbling random names. Your neighbors told us that you'd been acting strange for a few weeks. Coworkers said that you were unfocused and mumbling strange names at work. Some of the names they remember were Buster and, I think, Sophie. Do you know any people with those names?'

"Sophie and Buster are my cats, at least some of them."

"Interesting. We've had you on some medication and you're slowly getting better. You seem to be more in touch with reality. You'll need to stay with us for a few weeks to finish your treatments. You should notice a difference from the medication in a week or so."

Later that day I sat around a circle of people, some in gowns, and some in regular clothes. Each person talked in turn, telling a story about his or her life. After one person finished, everyone else sitting around the circle smiled and nodded. When it was my turn, someone asked me about cats. How they knew about my cats, I didn't know. It seemed natural to tell them the whole story—from the name of each cat to the food bills to the escape plan. I cried when I told them about the expenses from all those cats and how the expenses had become a huge stress. They all nodded and I continued the story. I told them that sometime last week, maybe last week; Sophie told me that six cats wanted to escape. In order to help them escape, I planned to leave the back door open when I went to bed and those who wanted to leave could be gone. I shook my head at the group, puzzled that I never asked Sophie where they were going or why they wanted to leave. As I told the story, the memory came back as so clear, so real. I giggled and looked at the woman next to me. That seemed impossible, didn't it, cats talking...? All the people in the circle smiled and nodded as if they understood completely.

The leader nodded, "Yes, we all know that cats don't talk, but we believe that YOU heard your cats talking."

"I don't know what's real anymore—when I'm here with you, the story of my cats escaping seemed like a dream, but when it happened, it was so real."

I went to group twice a day for the next two weeks and each time I told the same story, really in the same words. After hearing myself tell the story repeatedly, gradually I started to doubt that the cats really talked. One of the men in the group said that the medication was working. The psychiatrist visited me in my room twice more and congratulated me on the progress I'd made in the group. He said he'd increased my medication, and that if I continued getting better, I might be ready to go home in a week or so.

I knew the days of the week from the white board in my room and three weeks after admission, my brother took me home. The doctor felt that with medication I could manage at home alone with periodic checks by family.

It was good to be home. As I opened the front door, twelve sets of yellow eyes stared at me. It was as if I'd walked into a room where everyone stopped talking at once, because they had been talking about me. None of the cats spoke, but I assumed they wondered where I'd been. Their litter boxes were full, and their food dishes empty. Their little cat eyes were pitiful as they looked up and rubbed their bodies against my legs. I hurried to feed them and clean the lumpy litter boxes. The next day, everything seemed back to normal, except that there were some cats missing. I started to wonder if there had been an escape and tried to remember if I'd left a door open before the mental break. Was it all a dream?

A week later, I was driving home from work in the rain and saw a wet cat beside the road. I had to take him in, just to get him dry, and let him recover for a few days at home. It was Rudy. He looked scraggly and worn, but after a few days of rest and his favorite canned cat food, he was back to normal.

Sophie waited a few days for him to recover before she got the story. That afternoon she spilled the story to me. When I think about it, it was not strange that only Sophie could talk because she was a cat with a special gift. Rudy had told her that the outside was different— a risky, cold place— and that he couldn't handle the uncertainty.

A day after the escape, Buster gave them all a talk about freedom and started planning for their future. He heard from a tabby in an alleyway that there was steady work on the west coast in commercials. The last Rudy knew was that the bunch of them hopped a bus and headed for the coast.

Sophie told me all the remaining cats were glad Buster had gone to live his dream. As she cuddled in my lap, we wished him well and agreed that if there ever was a cat suited for commercials, it was Buster.

JOAN SPARKS

I love to clean on Tuesdays. No one gets married on a Tuesday, and the day is quiet except for an occasional sudden death, or nearly as bad, a serious accident. This past Tuesday was anything but quiet. I'm Pastor Joseph to my parishioners, Joe to my friends, and Puddin' Head to my old Divinity school classmates. I'm an experienced man of the cloth.

In late morning, a well-dressed young woman opened the front door, looked around to see if anyone was in the church, and started walking toward the front. I was cleaning behind the altar and should have spoken in order to alert her someone was there. Instead of speaking, I popped out from behind the altar and rushed the length of the aisle from the sanctuary to the nave. She was startled by a 250-pound man in red shorts and a Motley Crew T- shirt charging at her and she stepped back and held the top of the pew to brace herself.

She was smartly dressed in a pale blue, lightweight suit and had stylish blond hair, minimal makeup, and small pearl earrings dangling just below the edge of her hair - mid thirties I'd guess.

"Hello," I said, winded from the rushing. "How can I help you?" A smile started at her blue-green eyes and continued to her sparkling teeth. "I'm just in town for a short time and saw this pretty little church. I thought it would be fun to see the inside. Is this your church?" She was kind not to mention my outfit.

"Yes, I'm the pastor, Joe Delaney. Thank you for coming in to visit our church. We offer anyone a welcoming place for rest and contemplation. You're welcome to join us for services on Sunday or just look around if you prefer. Excuse my clothes, I was just cleaning behind the altar, and you caught me at my worst."

She offered her hand and smiled at the Motley Crew shirt. "No problem, I wear the same kind of clothes when I'm cleaning. Your church is charming. How long have you been pastor here? "

"Just over twenty years next month, a special anniversary; before that, I was in Crossville."

"I'm pleased to meet you, Joe. I'm Joan, Joan Sparks. I hope you don't mind my using your first name. Did I hear that your name was Delaney? I have a reason for asking other than familiarity. Delaney is an uncommon name in this part of the country. Did you grow up in Marsden? I hope I'm not prying if I ask if you have a brother." Many words, but spoken slowly with a hint of a Yankee accent.

"My home place is just outside Marsden, about a mile north of where we're standing. That's odd that you would ask about my brother. His name is Thomas, but I haven't see Tommy in over forty years. Do you know him?"

"Yes…yes I know him. I owe him a debt of gratitude I can never repay. I never got to tell him how much I appreciated his help."

"I'm not sure we're talking about the same Tommy. You said you had a gratitude you can never repay - only a few words, but a lot of meaning. It has to be an interesting story for you to come all the way to Marsden hoping someone might know a man named Tommy Delaney.

We sat in the front pew, and I gathered my thoughts. "Tommy left Marsden at sixteen and like older brothers, he was my hero. There was a bitter argument with dad, and Tommy left before dawn that next morning. Mom later told me what I'd suspected; the fight was the culmination of Tommy flexing his muscles as a young adult and my father trying to rein him in. I overheard hateful words from both of them that neither would take back. My last memory is of him turning right at the highway. He must have gotten a ride and after that, he disappeared into the world. As far as I know, he never contacted Mom. I went off to school, then to Divinity school, and was chosen by God to minister to the good people of Marsden. Mom and Dad died and Tommy may be dead, because I've always felt I was alone. Now you show up with news about Tommy. What can you tell me about his adventures?"

"Can we go someplace more private? My story is personal and the telling may take some time. I'd hate to have one of your parishioners come in to pray and overhear the conversation."

"Certainly, come to my office in the annex and we can talk."

I offered a chair and pulled up my office chair to face her, then leaned forward to match my body language to hers. She gathered her thoughts to tell the story and looked about to cry, so I extended my hand. She took it, linking us in a pastoral bond between strangers.

"I met your brother about a year ago. My husband left me six months before to take up with some big-breasted office bimbo, but I don't mean to imply that I'm bitter or anything. I hope you don't find my language offensive. I invested nineteen years in his career with boring office gatherings and sucking up to his bosses. In an instant, that investment was gone. At his office parties, I was expected to be a social drinker, maintaining the facade. I was the good wife nursing a single glass all evening. After he left me, I let things slide in my life, maybe out of anger, maybe to lessen the pain. Vodka was great for lessening pain. My drinking accelerated before I realized it from a bottle a week to a bottle every few days. After a few months, the divorce papers were delivered by a sheriff's deputy. To celebrate, I downed a bottle.

My girlfriends all knew the history and looked the other way with my drinking, calling it situational. They understood their husbands might find someone newer and that they might have the same problems. The day after I signed the papers they suggested we go to a neighborhood party a few blocks away to get out of the house. I've always been an angry drunk, and as the night went on and I drank more, I took my anger out on them. There was a scene, yelling, and tears, and I accused one friend of trying to seduce my husband. These were my last friends, those who'd stuck with me since he left and usually tolerated my emotions. This time my insults to them were personal. These girls had reached the end of their tolerance and left me drunk and passed out on the couch. Most of the guests had gone and the hosts were uncomfortable with an angry drunk, but considerate enough to ask if I wanted to stay over in the guest bedroom. I yelled some insult and thought I could walk home, but fell in the hallway after a few steps.

There was only one person still at the party; your brother Tommy, as it turns out and he was helping the hosts clean up. The host asked if Tommy could drive me home, I nodded consent and he propped me in the front seat as we stumbled to the car. Common sense was buried under alcohol and I'm fortunate I wasn't raped or killed by a stranger, but at the time, none of those things mattered. I woke up in a strange bed, wearing the clothes I wore to the party and nursing a colossal hangover. Moan - moan - headache - leather tongue trying to remember the night. I was on top of the comforter in a tidy guest room. Luckily, I had not vomited."

"A bad situation, but you're here today looking very different. What happened?"

"You're right, I am different. I saw the bottom of my life in that guestroom and knew with certainty that if I continued drinking, it would kill me. Over that day, I knew that my world had to turn around if I was going to choose to live. As I crawled into the kitchen that first evening, Tommy smiled and offered something to eat. My stomach was a mess. He started me on a cracker and apple juice mixture, but after a taste, I gagged. He helped me back to the guest room where I slept until morning. I don't know if you've ever had a soul-punishing experience like a hangover, but it is the lowest a person can sink.

The next morning when I came out, Tommy was in a recliner by the window and put down his blue book as I flopped onto the couch. "Are you feeling any better? Maybe you can try to get some liquids in to hydrate you. I've found that crackers - I prefer dry Ritz washed down with water or dilute apple juice - are the least nauseating after a serious bender, and I speak from long experience," he said.

"Now that some of the alcohol has worked its way out, I have so many questions. Who are you? Where am I? What day is this? Why am I here? When can I get a drink?"

"One at a time. My name is Tom Delaney. You're at my house, just a short distance from the party last nighty, you're safe, and it's Tuesday morning about nine o'clock."

"Damn, what happened from the party on Sunday night until now?"

"You drank way too much alcohol is what happened. Your body takes time to burn up all that alcohol. You're here because I can't let you go into the world until more of the alcohol has gone. Those are the basics. No drinks though - I'm sorry. I don't keep alcohol in the house."

"Joan, I'm sorry to interrupt you. You said Tom Delaney was this man's name. There must be more than a few men named Tom Delaney in North Carolina. How did you know this man was related to me?"

"Not as hard as you might think. Above the bed in the guest room was a large blue and yellow school pennant: Go Marsden Wildcats. It didn't take long to find Marsden and to confirm that the high school mascot was a wildcat. I looked up the name Delaney in Marsden, there was only one and this church was your address."

"A true detective. Let's get back to the story."

"I stayed with Tom during withdrawal. Those were the worst days of my life. He watched over me the entire time and accepted my anger, my sweating, my fevers, my vomiting, the pain in every muscle, my shakes, and my hallucinations. He cleaned my throw up and put me to bed after the worst every day. Each night in the darkness, I ranted at monsters and dark creatures coming at me from every shadow. I swore at him, called him every name I could think of, accused him of keeping me a prisoner and screaming that I'd report him for molesting me as soon as I got out of the hellhole he called a house. He didn't say anything about the mess or the abuse and his silence made me want to hurt him more. I started calling him names again, new ones this time and more hurtful, impugning his manhood and his mother. After five days, I woke up in the bedroom and saw the sun shining through the window and it was the first time in a long time that cared about the sunlight - tired but sober. I still felt sick but alive again."

"Withdrawal is a terrible experience. I've helped parishioners, and I marvel at how alcohol can take away a person's dignity. I've never seen an exorcism, but I think it must be a little like withdrawal. I can relate to your suffering."

"I never want to go through that pain again. As you might guess, Tom told me about AA and took me to my first meeting. I hated it, with all the stories by drunks and their ridiculous belief in a higher power, but he'd kept taking me. One man at the meeting talked about how much his sponsor had helped him. After a few meetings, I asked Tom if he would be my sponsor. His response surprised me."

"No Joan, it would be a bad idea for me to be your sponsor. You need a woman to be your sponsor and your support, but not your friend. Unless your sponsor watches carefully, you will become dependent. In the program, a sponsor is your guide to working the twelve steps, someone you can call anytime you feel the urge to drink, and someone you can be totally honest with about all the bad things you've done in your life. A sponsor listens without judging, but she is not your social friend. I would not be able to understand your pain."

"After a few more meetings, I realized that I have to start each day fighting the challenge to drink. Tommy got me started, but I know that constant will power and the support of friends are the only things that separate me from passing out drunk. The debt I owe Tommy is his faith in me, blind faith in me as a person without knowing me except as a passed-out drunk."

"I moved home and called Tommy every day for his support. I found a meeting for women and met my sponsor. She has been a jewel. Tommy and I met for lunch twice a week and talked about our lives. He shared that he'd been sober for three years and still called his sponsor every time he felt the urge to take that first drink. Of course I loved the man for all that he'd done."

"Wonderful. I'm so glad you found the right road. I'm hoping that Tommy will come back into the story now that you've told me so much about his kindness."

"No, Joe. He cannot come back to the story. Tommy was killed by a drunken driver as he left his regular meeting last week. I never told him how much he changed my life. After the funeral, I vowed to find you and tell you his story."

Both of us were silent for a long time, crying soft tears and looking away, each in their own world, but strangers closer through Tommy.

"Thank you for coming and for sharing Tommy's kindness. A part of you must believe that Tommy was sent by a higher power to rescue you."

"I do believe in help from that higher power. That belief and my sponsor will let me face another day without alcohol. Now that I've told you the story, I feel as if I've been able to share my gratitude and that it is somehow linked to Tommy. If my experience helps you find peace about your brother, it has been worth coming."

"Your visit has helped more than you know. God works in mysterious ways and your story renews my mission as a minister. Joan, please let me know when his stone is placed. I'd like to tell him about my life, about the parts he missed. He was a special man.

ELLIE AND ETHAN

"Is there any greater tribute to a woman than to recall her at her loveliest, a memory frozen in time? She will be beautiful forever, or for at least as long as you have memory."

Anonymous

Ellie's diary

August 2010

Monday

This is my first entry in this diary.

I'm frustrated and hurt. I suspect Ethan is lying and has been lying for some time, but it's hard to believe. This morning, in bed with my suspicions, my mind tumbled over the puzzle of how the man next to me, the man I'd been happy with for fifty years, could start lying. If I were gentle, I might call them untruths, but underneath they are lies. Any lie is a deception and every woman knows that after the first deception, no matter how trivial, things most often go down an unhappy road.

Ethan has always been a moral man, an admired church-going man in a town with many churches. He is respected in the community, a modern day Atticus Finch. People stop him on the street to talk about the events of the day, often looking to him as a compass in their personal storm. He is the kind of man who listens twice as much as he talks. I never thought lying was in his nature.

The first lie that I caught was his story that he hadn't been to town in more than a week, even though my friend Jeannie had seen him talking to a woman on Main Street just the day before. Jeannie claimed not to know the woman, perhaps to spare me any embarrassment. After that shocker, any subsequent lies seemed trivial, usually about where he'd been during the day or whom he talked with on the phone. I kept my own counsel and waited for him to come clean. Instead, his deceptions became bolder. Several times now, he has been gone for an afternoon without any explanation, and friends have commented on seeing him in an unfamiliar part of town.

Tuesday

My anger continues, and I've been unsure how to confront him to get some kind of an explanation.

Today I remembered that lying runs in his family. Uncle Wilmot, a con man in Western Carolina, narrowly escaped jail because of Ethan's quiet intervention. Now Ethan is showing a pattern of lies and deceit similar to Wilmot. I replayed conversations of the past, wondering how many times he's lied before: lied to me, lied to people he knew. I read that some liars can't help it, feeding on lies and believing them even after the truth is discovered.

October 2010

It's been several months since my last entry, and I've checked and rechecked Ethan's stories. What I thought was calculated lying has only been his innocent forgetfulness. Relief! I'm glad he's not been lying, but now I feel guilty about blaming him so quickly and questioning fifty years of trust by my reckless suspicions. I wonder if this forgetfulness is due to his aging.

In other parts of our lives, things are normal; he's as attentive and as affectionate as always. Each day I find new signs that his memory is failing. I accept that now and so I interpret everything differently. Maybe he will recognize his memory lapses so that we can discuss them. That discussion will be painful because of his pride, but in fifty years of marriage, we've shared many painful things—we've shared and we've gotten through them.

January 2011

It's after the holidays and I've become convinced that Ethan's memory is deteriorating faster. He is not normal. Over the holidays, he's become withdrawn from the kids and grandkids, and is not the usual vibrant conversationalist at family dinners. His irritability is higher, and at least once a week he explodes at me over minor things that would have passed unnoticed a year ago. He's stopped meeting with his friends at Julesky's and wanders around the house as if he's looking for something. In the mornings, he sits in his chair and looks through the paper, but I'm not sure he's even reading. He shuffles the pages too much, and he's stopped doing the daily crossword.

Today after our walk, he emptied his pockets and sorted through each item on the table, even sniffing a key holder. He asked me to smell the leather holder, and when I did, he nodded, looking to me for approval. I held back my tears.

March 2011

In the three months since my last entry, he has regressed to sitting in his chair all day and staring out the window. I decided to call the children, hoping they might spend a few days with him and give me their impressions.

I called Jamie, our oldest, and explained my concern. His first word was shit. I don't like that he's become such a foul-mouth with his fancy city job. After my update on his father and my worries, he sighed and said he'd call me back after checking his calendar. Some big business deal was on his mind. He thought I was overreacting but promised he'd be home after the deal was done. He assured me that Dad would be back to normal soon enough.

Next, I call Holly, our middle child, a girl who marches to her own drummer. She listened to the story and suggested that Dad was not eating right. She'd read in *Today's Health* about vitamin deficiencies in older adults that could cause strange behavior. Vitamin B12 levels were often low in older men, and she suggested that before I got even more worried and took him to the doctor, I should add a multivitamin every morning and, for good measure, an extra dose of Vitamin B12. "It can't hurt," she added. She was rushing out the door for her annual nutrition conference in Europe. She promised to check back when she got home about whether he improved on the vitamins.

Then I called Violet, our most sensible child. Thankfully, she promised to come home in two days. She could arrange for someone to drive the children to their after-school activities, and Jason was due back from his business trip in the morning. There was a flight on Wednesday. We agreed that I would pick her up at the airport and ask Dad to ride with me. That night I think Ethan must have known I had called the children, and he was unusually quiet after dinner.

Violet got home Wednesday evening. Ethan went to the airport with me, and at Marsden's tiny two-gate airport, he didn't recognize anything. He was surprised to see Violet, but at least he recognized her. On the walk to the car, everything seemed normal as we all chatted, and he asked about the occasion for her to come home. Ever the diplomat, she said she had missed us both and wanted some good home-cooked meals. On the ride home, Ethan started into a rambling story about different styles of shoes, and how did a woman decide on the kind of shoes she needed. Violet and I looked at each other and wondered where that had come from.

She was worried from the moment she saw him, and even more so when he came downstairs the next morning dressed in a nice dress shirt, pajama bottoms, and slippers. She and I talked it over all of Thursday and decided it was time for him to see the doctor. Doc Jordan had been our doctor for many years and knew us both well. At the office, Ethan seemed normal and spoke to the reception staff and nurses as he always had, smiling with his usual winks and flirting. When they called him back for vitals, I went with him. If Ethan thought that odd, he did not mention it.

Ethan's diary

November 2010

Ellie thinks there's something wrong with me, but I don't think there is anything serious, just minor aches and pains that come with being 73 years old. The only thing I've noticed is that my sense of smell has somehow become wrong. Some days I smell odd odors like burning wood and lilacs and buttered popcorn, all mixed up in a cloud of confusion. I love each of the smells, but they only last a second or two, and it's hard to appreciate any of them. The combination is nauseating. Something's not right, but I'm sure it's something minor and it will pass.

My memory has become a little worse. I can't remember what we had for breakfast or lunch. I've noticed other things, too, like fumbling for a word, forgetting names of people I know, or not being able to solve a crossword. I know getting old makes brain cells work slower, but the memory thing is a bother. I'll have to do some reading about this.

Tuesday November 20, 2010

Apparently, there are many causes for memory loss in older people, but one cause popped out at me right away—Alzheimer's disease. My friend Raymond has the big A, and it's devastating to see a part of him slip away each day. Now he doesn't even know me. When I think more about it, I'm sure that my mind is weaker and the symptoms are getting worse. I'm worried that I'll lose that most precious of qualities, the ability to think and to communicate. If that's my fate, all I can say is…damn, what a pickle. Maybe that's my end game if it's Alzheimer's that's causing my memory changes.

Just in case, I will get our financial affairs in order over the next few weeks. Barry Graham specializes in elder law and can handle all the details. Elder law, ha…just another way for lawyers to make money, interpreting routine law for old people. I want to get all that technical stuff done while I still can.

Wednesday November 21, 2010

I don't know how much longer I might be able to write like this before I sink too deep. I know you'll read this diary eventually, Ellie. If I have Alzheimer's, maybe you'll see that this diary is a way for me to write about those feelings I never told you. First, I want to tell you how much I love you and have loved you from the first time I saw you walking on the street in Chapel Hill. That memory comes back as clear as yesterday, your walk and your smile, the color and the smell of the leaves. I thank God for our time together.

As my mind becomes feeble, please know that somewhere deep inside I feel our love. Our love will endure, somehow, a treasure for the rest of my days. I've always depended on you and your common sense. I hope I've told you often enough how you've made me a better man. All these feelings need to be written down, now, while I still can. Not saying the right words often enough, the loving words, is my fault. I've read articles about the disease and books by family members of Alzheimer's patients. Everyone describes their sadness as the spark fades from their loved one's eyes. A terrible fate, but it may be that those are the cards I've been dealt. You've always complimented me on my smile, although maybe it's just your way of being kind. In this time of trial, let's focus on a smile as something positive. I will do my best as my mind fades to smile whenever I can. No matter how bad things get, know that my smile is for you, and that I'm struggling to show you a glimpse of my old self.

Thursday December 1, 2010

They say someone my age should be sure their financial things are in order, to take care so that those you leave behind don't have to worry about finances. Don't worry. In our 50 years together, I've seen to it that you've never had to pay a bill or even write a check. I spoiled you. After I'm gone, you'll find a rich old man to take care of you. You still have your looks, and you are a wonderful companion, so it should be easy. You've had an easy life, what more could you ask for? In these days, you should be able to put up with a little memory lapse by an old guy every now and then, at least out of kindness.

I'm finding it hard to get words collected in a sentence and had to edit this entry to clear up the stupid mistakes in grammar or wording—you should have seen the first draft. I hope you can read it with all the scratch marks.

January 2011

This morning, after the kids left from the holidays, you and I had a yelling match about my forgetfulness. Really, I did most of the yelling, and you listened. You said I had a short fuse. A bunch of noisy kids running around the house is stressful to anyone. Short fuse indeed! You badger me every hour of every day. Just yesterday, you walked out of the room just because I'd forgotten the name of our youngest grandchild. Michael, Michael, that's it—it came to me just now. It was just on the edge of my mind. I yelled the name down the stairs to show you my memory is as sharp as it's always been. Keeping track of the names of each of the children, the six grandchildren, all our friends in Marsden, and all the people I've met in a lifetime is a task. At 73, I should be allowed a little liberty. I think you're starting to get demented the way you run around the house, checking everything as if you've misplaced it. Now that I think about it, those dullards at Julesky's have become so boring I'm going to stop seeing them.

Now that we're being honest, I think you've been spending too much time at that shoe store downtown. How many shoes can a woman need, and why do you always have to stop there when you go downtown? The guy who runs the store, Dickie Roosevelt, moved south 20 years ago when we did, but only opened the store about 5 years ago after his wife died. I've always thought the store was a front for him to meet women, and now you've fallen into his trap. I can't find a way to ask you without provoking one of those yelling matches that have become all too common. I know you're not that kind of girl, at least not that I've ever suspected, but Dickie has a charm I don't have. Truth be known, I think you've had your eye on Dickie for years, and you've both been planning to get my money and go on a fancy cruise around the world. You've always said you wanted to go on a long cruise, but I wouldn't go, afraid of seasickness.

Anyway, all this yelling and tantrums came on today because I forgot that grandkid's name. I'm entitled to a bit of forgetfulness with so much to worry about, and for good measure, I'm entitled to a good dose of ornery every so often. I hope to God that you get to go on your damn cruise before you get more forgetful or Dickie will leave you for somebody younger.

March 2011

Ellie took me to see Doc Jordan for my annual physical. He's a good egg and pronounced me in great health for a man of 73. He said my body and heart were better than average. I've noticed that he's become a bit strange since I saw him a year ago. He seems to forget things, and I wonder how he can still practice. He's pushing 70 and used to smoke pretty heavily. During our interview, he kept asking me questions, silly questions as if he'd forgotten where he was and needed my help to clarify reality. Who is the president, what's the date, where are we now, and questions like that. With his failing memory, it's only a matter time until he'll have to close up his practice. I hope he closes before he hurts somebody. Where will we all go for medical care? I know I'm not going to that youngster at the end of town, Jamie something. He's only been here a year, and he'd never understand me. The good old days are gone when we were friends with all the doctors in town. They never charged us for visits and filled any medicines we needed from their office. One thing about Doc Jordan, he always hired pretty nurses.

Lately Ellie's become as slippery as sin, going outside to talk on the phone, going out to lunch with her friends, and just the other night calling the children. She never used to do that. We had a nice visit with Violet when she was here, and then she went back to her brood.

Ellie's diary

March 2011

The visit to Doc Jordan confirmed my suspicions. I knew he would diagnose Alzheimer's, but the word scared the shit out of me. I have to hold myself together every day because Ethan's memory is not only gone, but he's become paranoid and spiteful. He talked to Jim Jordan like never before, just being rude. While Ethan sat in the waiting room, Jim gave me a realistic picture, telling me things would get much worse. The way they've been going, they would worsen in just a few months. He suggested I meet with the children to decide if we could manage Ethan's care at home or if he would need a care facility. Jim wants to try some medication but admitted that it only delays the inevitable. He felt there's only so much of his personality that can come back.

Tuesday April 13, 2011

Last night I looked at Ethan asleep, lying on his back with his legs crossed, his hands gently folded over his chest, and his nose pointed at the ceiling. Only his slow regular breathing assured me he was not positioned that way by an undertaker. If I turned toward him, our eyes would be a hand's width apart, but the darkness would hide our faces. What was he thinking?

I can't help wondering about the days ahead, each day slowly getting worse with no hope of recovery. How many days can I endure? If there is a hell on earth, this surely must be it—never again looking forward to anything except his passing. I've started praying that he will go first, quietly in the night, called home by a merciful God. What irony that the rest of his body is healthy.

I've started to worry about my health. If I get sick, who will take care of him? What if I died in a car accident, and he survived? I pray that I'll have the strength to keep this as our home, his home, and that my health hold on long enough.

The children encouraged me to move him to a facility devoted to Alzheimer's care. I know they're thinking of me and the stress of caregiving. With common sense, they point out that expert care in such a facility would be better for both of us. A home, even with caring staff, is not his home and would be a miserable place to die. Reluctantly, I've started visiting care facilities. The staff tries to be friendly and supportive, but each one is like a fancy hotel with a bunch of people who don't know each other. One nurse told me that many clients fall and break a hip. Ethan trips over his slippers.

Who will watch out for that and what would happen if he had a broken hip? Care homes are expensive and we can afford the expense for a while. My heart says I need to care for him at home until it becomes more than I can handle.

Yesterday I came across the diary he'd written, read, and reread his account. The dry humor and resignation to his fate was vintage Ethan. When I read his touching comments about us, about me, I wanted to ask about his feelings, but he sat motionless, staring out the window. All the answers were forever locked in his head. I cried softly because I would never know.

His last entry was a few weeks ago, written in barely legible handwriting...

Can't write can't think feel like crying smil.

AT THE END OF THE HALL

My name is Josephine, and when it comes to religion, I'm practical. God lives in my world, and I live in His, but we've reached an agreement about our roles. I don't believe in using God for a wish list. He knows my needs, but I'm sure he laughs at my wishes. He is merciful and kind, but as far as granting wishes, I've never seen much on that account. When people have troubles, they turn to God; if he doesn't answer, they turn to their second choice, the devil, and expect an answer more to their liking. People rarely return to God with thanks. Its tough being God.

I have plenty of troubles at 76, mostly aches and pains and dealing with stupid people. My latest trouble started a month ago with chest pain. An occasional pain happens, but when the pain comes more often, I call my doctor. The short story is that there is a large tumor in my chest, in my lung actually and there is not much to be done. The doc wanted testing, and I needed to spend a few days in the hospital.

After completing the admission paperwork, a nice young girl wheeled me to a quiet room at the end of the hall. It was believed that my condition was terminal. Nurses were considerate and caring, yet everyone knew their best efforts could only provide comfort and not healing. There is something about the last room on the hall. Nurses know when a patient is admitted whether they are a troublemaker, a screamer, a loud talker, or have noisy children—any of these take a lot of time for a busy nurse. Patients who will not misbehave, usually the terminal ones, are settled into the last car on the train at the end of the line. They lie in their room at the end of the hall, mostly reflecting, until they either go home or die.

There was only one test on the afternoon of my admission, and a few friends visited that evening. Close friends stand in the dim hallway at the end of visiting hours, quietly talking about how I looked. They must not know my hearing is excellent. Some are not charitable about my appearance, as if I had the leisure of getting dolled up. My friend Joyce was the usual brand of visitor, uncomfortable in a sick room and covering it by wearing minimal makeup and making her full lips pale to match my complexion. She sat still in the chair and alternately pouted or affected a fabricated smile. That was her hospital face. She tried to hide her nervousness, but I felt it. As she had done during every lunch we'd ever had, she spent the first half hour telling me about her general problems. For the second act, she started into her specific problems. The latest crisis was that her neighbor's dog messed on her lawn and dug up her garden. As I listened, I thought uncharitable thoughts. Why does she have to tell me that mess now? I don't care about the damn dog, and I had to hold back from telling her to take her problems and put them in the long line behind all of mine and wait to see which I'll be considering. I was charitable and didn't tell her. She left after her record had finished playing and I had time to reflect after visiting hours ended.

The room at the end of the hall was conducive to deep thought, about God and about how you've lived your life. The cycle of life was an endless balance of old and unhealthy people leaving the earth and young and healthy people arriving. Life could end suddenly, a merciful and quick transition between living and then not.

However, life could also end slowly with a terminal illness like mine as a slow, often painful process with lots of time to replay the highlights of a life and the regrets. Dying fast or dying slow, if we had a choice, which would we choose?

Early the next morning in the darkness, I wondered about the kind of voice God used when he called souls to him at the end. It was probably soft and calm, reassuring after the stress of dying. I imagined an angel softly saying, "This way please" as the soul glided toward a soft white light. On the other side of the universe, the devil's minion called to lost souls in a voice filled with despair and infinite sadness, but using the same words "this way please" and pointed down a path to a deep black chasm. As I read the papers with all the mass killings, by accident or intention, I've thought that the devil must prefer to harvest souls in a crowd in order to save trips. Although every soul was worth a trip, multiples had to be more pleasurable. Rarely he missed one as it floated out of his cold fingers and back to life, a plane crash survivor for example, and he must regret not being able to take them. He probably shrugged off the disappointment and moved to his next appointment. He knew all would be called eventually and he expected to get the majority.

At the end, God would appear and speak to the sorted souls. We could no longer resist him as we did in life. No matter what the judgment, God always spoke at the end. Better to know him during life than to resist him. Those who didn't know any better walked through life afraid of God.

In the early hours of the morning, I realized that the dead were not so far away. Friends and relatives were with me just on the other side of the hospital wall. If I concentrated in the quiet, I could make out their words—encouraging words, supportive words. Would I die in this place with my last memories coming before the light of another morning?

I suspected that Death was approaching. I was a woman coming into a dark room with the door closing and no visible exit, trapped in the unfamiliar room, frightened, and enveloped by darkness as the door finally closes. Memories flooded back, and I wondered if I had done enough, learned enough, helped enough, prepared enough, and I knew that any thoughts were useless; the time of learning and preparing had gone by, and whatever was to be would be.

It was close to sunrise when a light slipped under my closed eyelids and interrupted my reflections. It was the purest bright white, soft but unwavering. The light seemed to float at the end of spiraling intertwined threads and continued off into the distance. I could not see an end. Surely, this must be the angel calling. Was I ready?

As I opened my eyes, the light cleared, and I saw the face of my doctor, smiling. He had contacted the National Institutes of Health had some good news. There was hope for treating my tumor with a new medication that had been effective in preliminary clinical trials. Although the treatments were still investigational, was I interested? It would be a chance to live.

After too short a time for any reasoning, I told him I did not want treatment. My family and my best friends had gone before me, and I heard them on the other side of the wall the previous night, calling me. It would not be long.

God, please guide me home.

MY SOUL MATE

I'll tell you a story that gives me the most fear, because it will be my undoing at judgment day. It's said that any sin can be forgiven, but forgiveness requires repentance, and I cannot repent. No matter how I squirm or twist, the slimy fingers of the sin are around my throat, pulling me back into the memory of what I've done. If calling down a curse is not a crime, it should be, because the results are as devastating. A curse is a silent crime committed with full knowledge and forethought.

I met Kerri at the annual garden party that first summer. Mother pronounced that the girl was little more than a dressed up drunken slut, but I thought my mother was being too harsh. However, at the garden party the following summer, Kerri was just one drink away from proving my mother right. That year James was her target, my James.

My given name is Elizabeth, Lizzie to my friends. Soon after I met James in college, he insisted on calling me Elizabeth. He said the formality engendered respect, and respect was how the relationship evolved. He was the first man who called me his soul mate and the only man I've believed. It's not that he was catch-your-breath gorgeous, but his flyaway muddy-colored hair and limpid blue eyes stirred me like no other man. James was indeed my soul mate, and we started planning for marriage, good jobs in Charlotte, and children.

I was devastated when he left, a slow, painful leaving with Kerri's easy sexuality pulling him closer each day until she'd captured him. After he announced he'd chosen her, not me, I looked for seclusion to forget my soul mate.

His leaving crushed my soul and my spirit. I was sick for weeks. It was an ugly sickness that resisted sleep, medication, food, or tears. Each day my soul was squeezed by pain.

I've had the past thirty years to reflect on him, and I still carry that sadness…but sadness is eased by knowing that he has suffered mightily, and that the curse has done its work.

After he left, I turned to God for solace. The church promised peace for my soul and recovery from my pain. All societal divisions vanished as God and the church elders treated everyone as a believer, no matter their sin or pain, and offered comfort to us all. I became the model of church involvement in bake sales, cleaning the church, and prayer groups. In the choir, I sang a good hymn, forcefully but off-key—an excellent crowd voice—and after the service, people would comment on my voice. I created an identity. If not for the influence of the church, I would have become a drunkard on a street corner in Marsden.

The church taught me that God constantly passes his loving eye over the world, taking in every thought and every action, now and forever. His mystery is knowing the outcome of every event and yet not intervening. He cares deeply for every being and does not interfere with their world of choices. I learned but did not believe. A merciful God could not assuage my anger. In desperation, I turned to the devil and eventually to magic. Magic and superstition filled a void that God did not abide.

My friend Elise doubted my superstition and my magic, but I assured her that the devil's superstition resides in each of us and he knows our weaknesses. Elise laughed at magic, but I convinced her that as time marches on, each day, there was either magic or luck. Maybe luck existed, but I'd never seen it. Good or bad happened as God randomly lifted his right hand or his left. There was no randomness in magic, only willful acceptance. After more wine than usual, Elise asked if magic included the ability to create a curse. Magic taught me that we all have the power of a curse deep within us but only lack the means to awaken it. I looked into her eyes and smiled, knowing that a curse was the only vehicle that allowed the wronged to avenge themselves. I sought out a witch outside of Varnamtown, learned a powerful curse, and paid her well for her knowledge. She advised me that such a curse should be used sparingly, reserved for those who deserved it most. James was the prime candidate.

The next night my room was dark except for three candles burning around the circumference of a circle as I invoked the dark spirits with the words and actions the witch had taught me. A lock of James's muddy-colored hair lay on the floor in the center to serve as the channel, and a stick of balsam fir incense, his favorite, burned beside it. Summer breezes floated through the room, and the candles flickered. When the time was right, I wished for ill will to him from that day forward: pain, sickness, bad dreams, mental instability, paranoia, loneliness, financial loss, and gum disease. When my wish was spoken, the candles flickered and went out. All was dark again with the lingering smell of balsam. I knew the curse had taken hold, and I smiled.

Moving back into normal life took considerable time. I looked toward a foggy and uncertain future and considered how I could get there. The days stretched ahead, one lonely tedious dawn and dusk after another. Gradually I passed through the cloud and met Lester, a good man, but not a soul mate. We married and found a kind of happiness and, eventually, financial independence. No children came, but we enjoyed each other's company. Years passed and Lester died after a long illness. I was alone—too late in life to start again. To combat the loneliness, I returned to the church with a healthier perspective, reestablished my place in the choir, and spent time in the ministry volunteering with friends. Although my friends were a blessing, I missed the close companionship and simple shared talk of marriage. I never regretted the life I could not live but have never enjoyed my life again. Occasionally, I thought about James.

As if in answer to my thoughts, I saw him in the grocery store early in the fall. We nodded, as people do who have not seen each other in thirty years, wondering what happened in the interval. I stopped to talk, anxious to hear what misfortunes had happened to my soul mate. He'd been married, his wife had died in an auto accident, and there were three grown children, two in prison and one nearly there. His hands were deformed by arthritis. He told his story with no emotion, just with resignation. In his blue eyes, I saw a glimpse of my soul mate, but I didn't feel love. He asked, and I told him my story, of Lester, of growing old in Marsden, and of my life in the church. My sadness lifted, hearing the details of his story, but I wanted him to suffer more—what about the sleeplessness, the pain, the financial ruin, and how were his teeth?

BAD WORDS

I couldn't stop it. Part primal scream and part cry of pain, the word passed my lips. Within milliseconds, events progressed from hammer to finger to pain and to my favorite curse word leaving my lips. I was assembling a project in the garage, a wooden shelf my Cub Scout den was having us build to surprise our parents. My mother was hanging clothes on the line and her hearing was perfect. Her maternal instincts responded to the cry, but more to the foul word. I'm sure she'd heard worse from my father, but the word coming from my nine-year-old mouth was unacceptable.

All day, every day, she patrolled our home and the perimeter of our yard alert to possible trouble; she usually found something that required yelling. No one ever counted the yells, but we suspected a minimum of three hundred times a day were needed to maintain order and discipline. She seldom used corporal punishment, but an occasional swat was not out of the question. Yelling was considered an appropriate reaction to anything outside her norm. Cursing, from anyone except my father, was a capital offense. Today, even before the word had settled in the air, she marched into the garage, took my arm, and dragged me into the downstairs bathroom. She grabbed a bar of soap from the sink, whatever was handy, and started the process called "washing your mouth out." This was her punishment for evils of speech, which included both cursing and any smart mouth talk. Several good swipes in the front of my mouth with the orange bar of Dial was the application phase, followed by a liberal rub back and forth across my back teeth. She changed hands for a better angle and delivered a good dose to my tongue from back to front. It didn't matter if I gagged. Just to be sure I got the message, she finished with light rubs along the under surface of my front teeth.

A light touch was needed to preserve the expensive orthodontia. After it was done, she nodded, then stood back to consider her work.

She considered the process to be a clean sweep, as if more foul language might be hanging out somewhere in my mouth and needed to be expunged. She followed the clean sweep with more yelling along the lines of "when will you learn that I won't tolerate that kind of talk in this house." Before she left the bathroom, she gave me a steady look in the mirror to make it clear the next time the punishment would be worse. She never told my father about the soap because he might have minimized the offense, but he knew something had gone down because of the tooth marks on the soap.

In the hierarchy of cursing, there was a minor group of words covering nonsexual body functions and a major group of words that invoked either God or the variety of colorful words describing sexual functions. At nine, my cursing was confined to the minor group but I'd heard them all. Only my neighborhood pals who went to public school used the major bad words, and they floated them in any conversation like badges of independence. In the Catholic faith, major foul language required confession, always on the next Saturday and without exception if the words involved blasphemy. Everyone knew that if you died before confessing a major sin, you'd rot in Hell for eternity, so forgiveness in the confessional was essential to clear the slate. A boy didn't want to take chances in case an airplane was to fall on his house or if he rode his bike off a cliff.

After mom left the room, I stood beside the sink with a soap-encrusted mouth and time to think about my use of bad words. Mostly I thought about the soapy taste. Dial had a distinctive taste, but the smell was nearly as powerful. From experience, I found it helpful to moisten my fingers with water and try to rub as much of the soap off my teeth as possible while holding my breath. Using a toothbrush didn't help because the soapy taste never quite left the bristles and left an unpleasant reminder. It took considerable rubbing and swishing to get the larger chunks out with lots of gagging and spitting. About ten good rinses cleared most of the soapy taste, but the smell hung on. By that time, my younger brother and sister were standing in the hall watching the action. My brother barely held in his laughter because he knew the details from personal experience. My sister was the curious one; she wanted to know how Dial tasted, had I swallowed any, and was I going to be belching up bubbles all day like on the cartoons. My sister was a good girl and never tasted soap.

The Catholic boys in the neighborhood knew about the ritual from regular encounters, while the public school crowd just laughed. Catholic parents believed that if children, usually boys, used foul language, it was the start of their slide down the short road to perdition. The corner store sold a lot of soap, mostly Dial.

A TALE OF DECEPTION

"Oh what a tangled web we weave when we practice to deceive"

Marmion Walter Scott

It was 1967. The Vietnam War and free love dominated the news. Religion was once again popular and people had money to donate to God or to God's agents and one of God's agents had a plan to harvest people's money. Crossville was a coastal town in North Carolina with enough Bible belt Christians to make the plan profitable. The man was Jimmy DeVane, lately of Baltimore Maryland, but when he came to Crossville, he was the preacher.

*****

They were in a prime location on the main road into town. Clifton and Mildred Smithson bought the Restful Inn twenty years ago and up until a year ago, Marsden was an up-and-coming place—a good stopping place to gas up and grab a bite on their way south to Crossville. All of their sixteen rooms were filled and there was a waiting list in the summer. The man they later found out was the preacher seemed different and Clifton felt it from their first meeting, but just how different was only later confirmed when the sheriff came looking. The man was too scraggly for a salesman, a wrinkled black suit hanging loose on his medium frame, dirty slick black hair, and his forehead thick with dust and sweat. Clifton was suspicious after the front door slammed behind him and the man started the easy small talk of a salesman. He was too friendly in a sleazy way.

"Good afternoon, I can see you have a fine establishment here and I wonder if you might have a room for the night," said the man.

"You've got good taste in motels, mister. Our rooms are clean, quiet and priced fair. We're convenient on the highway, but far enough back that you'll never hear traffic noise. We offer free hot coffee and a sweet roll in the morning."

"Well, that sounds like the best deal I've had all week. My business takes me along this corridor almost every month, and I've rarely had a need to stop, but today I find myself behind in my calls and have to rest up. I'm feeling a little sickly and don't want to push driving for another four hours. I have a little extra time, and if Marsden suits me, I may stay a few days to rest up and see the sights."

"Then our motel is the place for you. As I say, our rooms are clean and spacious with no road noise. I'm sorry you're feeling a bit sickly and I hope you'll be better by morning. Might I get your name for the register?"

"My friends call me the preacher, and since we're going to be doing business together, you are one of my friends."

"Well, Preacher, I'm Clifton, it's good to meet you. What kind of room do you need? We have singles, doubles, and then our largest room that we call the honeymoon suite—a king bed with a sitting room. Our best rooms are in the back and we just happen to have a double available. It'll be $29.95 plus tax per night, and even though check-in is 4:00 pm, I can let you check in now.

"Thank you, sir, that's mighty kind. I will take that room, and is it okay if I pay with cash?"

"Cash is the best commodity. The total is $31.68."

"Here's $32.00, sir. I'll need a receipt so I can claim a business expense, and you can keep the change for your trouble. If I decide to stay on, can I have the same room?"

"Thank you. Preacher, it's a pleasure doing business with a cash customer. I can block the room for three days and you let me know when you want to check out. What kind of business are you in?"

"I sell a little bit of this and little bit of that, bibles and such, and most of my time I spread the word of God. All my stock fits in the car, and I make a run to Chicago once a quarter and pick up enough bibles and pamphlets to refill the car. By the time I'm heading back to Chicago at the beginning of the next quarter almost everything is sold, and there is a good wad in my pocket that I contribute to the needy. Do you have a restaurant here on property, one with good home cooking? I prefer a thick juicy T-bone steak with mashed potatoes and corn, and if you have it, a big slice of hot apple pie with ice cream on the side."

"You're in luck, Preacher, Mildred is a fantastic cook, and if you tell us what time you'd like to eat, we'll have your favorites at a reasonable price."

"Thanks. I'm going to freshen up and take a nap. Can we say 7 o'clock for dinner?"

As this salesman walked away, I knew that he was no more a preacher than old Rover was a hunting dog.

The preacher was going with his preferred alias in this town. He decided that nearby Crossville would be his next con because it was the right size with the ideal combination of religious fervor and loose money. The Restful Inn was far enough north to let him work out the details in private. The revival con required a detailed setup and two paid staff members to be the most profitable. He'd thought about the fraternity of scam artists, confidence men, and cheaters at cards that worked the circuit along the Eastern seaboard and could call a friend to work any skill, but this would be a local job for local talent. Anyway, the preacher would be the main attraction.

That night the food was tasty, the room was quiet, and he slept the sleep of the damned, all good omens. After a shower last night, he looked in the mirror in the morning sunshine and saw a clean man with an easy smile. The smile made people trust him, especially women, who felt the appeal of his etched face. He had unusual delicate eyelashes that drew attention to his cold gray eyes, eyes that were a subtle warning about his character. Sunglasses were a good cover because most people remembered his smile and his voice and overlooked his eyes.

In Marsden, his outfit for scouting about town was local: casual jeans tucked into spit-shined boots and a short-sleeved blue cotton shirt. His lucky gold neck chain sparkled in the morning sun. The image suggested a man with experience—a man who knew what he wanted, but not the image of a preacher.

Fellow scam artists would call him a professional, a successful professional, in an occupation where not many can make that claim. In twenty years working up and down the east coast, in more than fifty towns between Baltimore and Florida, he'd never had trouble. He ran different cons suited to the town and the people. There was enough money in his pocket to live well and plenty more safely banked. In a typical town, the con took a few days and then he was gone. It was his professional pride that after a con, people never suspected they'd been conned.

In Marsden, he was recruiting for two associates to play their parts and not ask questions. The pay was good, and he expected never to see them after the con. He cruised down Main and parked the LeBaron in front of a restaurant at the far end of town. The hand-lettered sign inside the front window boasted the Best Breakfast in Town. As he walked through the front door, he nodded to the customers spread out between the counter and the tables and they looked up from their coffee before sharing a knowing smile with friends. They kept a curious eye out because this character was not from around there, but the outfit made him look like one of them.

*****

Between breakfast customers at the diner, Amy replayed her life. For most of her nineteen years, she had been a good girl, and life had unfolded to her advantage. At eighteen, she discovered the power of sex and as a farmer's daughter; she knew well that all males had the same urges. As a practical girl, she learned to combine men's urges and her sexual power to make some easy money. There were plenty of opportunities to practice with older men; they appreciated the attention and showed their appreciation by buying gifts. She learned to get gifts early, when a man's enthusiasm was at its highest. She never asked for cash, but most men learned that a few twenty-dollar bills would buy an enthusiastic smile, and often more. Flirting became a show, saying what a man wanted to hear and suggesting more. With older men, the show led to profitable casual sex, but with boys her age, the show was a waste—they had no money. The combination of a summer sundress, blonde hair, and minimal makeup—the innocent look—turned old men into children. Wielding sexual power became an addiction.

She worked to perfect an image and mixed snippets of movie clips to give a blend of exotic and aflame, brazen and irresistible. She practiced the image on men in nearby towns because there were rarely any men worth the trouble at the diner.

Then she met the preacher, and her life turned upside down. As he came through the front door of the diner for breakfast that first morning, she brought him a cup and a pot and sat it on the edge of the table.

"Morning, what can I get ya?"

"Two eggs, wet, sausage on the side, and home fries if you've got them. Bring a bowl of grits, dry white toast, and some strawberry jam. Do you have a local paper?"

"The paper comes out on Tuesdays. I have one from last week, but the next one won't be until next Tuesday late morning. There's never much news here. I can't guarantee the paper will be complete. The comics and the crossword puzzle go first, but what's left will probably have most of the local news, what little there is, with the classified section if you want it. There may be some spills on it."

"No matter, just so it's clear enough to read about Marsden."

As he shoveled eggs onto his toast, the preacher reviewed his plan. The eggs were perfect, runny like he ordered and he looked around the diner to pass the time. He watched a red-eyed fly walk across the counter and through his saucer. It was unusual enough to take notice because the fly had no fear, as if it was accustomed to wandering through food. Eventually, the waitress brought a stained newspaper. As he'd suspected, there were no opportunities for a quick con, and he saw no reason to swat the fly.

After some reflection, he settled on the classic religious con with a fast turnaround and two local partners. The con needed a pretty young girl. This waitress was pretty enough in a wholesome sort of way and, with the right clothes and makeup, she could offer the view he needed for the religious crowd. In any town, there were rebellious girls, good looking enough to attract attention, and fast enough to satisfy his needs. He had a gift for spotting advantages. This innocent girl would work out as people's first impression and her smiling eyes would complete the image. She would have to appear shiny new in her role of greeting and seating the faithful. This waitress's had brown eyes, almost black because of the lashes, and her blonde hair and healthy complexion created a look that came at you frankly, a candid boldness mixed with an innocence that made you like her from that first look. Men would love her, and women would not feel threatened by her. He smiled at the waitress and started his pitch.

"Miss, let me introduce myself. People call me the preacher. I don't look like one now, but my specialty is healing, usually at revivals, but wherever the Lord calls me. I can make a deaf man hear and a blind woman see, and that's just the start of it. Let me just get right to it. I can feel that God sent me in this diner to find you, to ask you to help in my work. The Lord has guided me here to preach and heal down in Crossville and I need a young woman to help with the believers. I can feel that you have the spirit of the Lord. When any of us are called, we have the choice of answering the Lord, or of turning away. The Lord needs you—I need you—to help spread His spirit in Crossville and I hope you won't turn away. The revival will last two days. I can pay good money for your work, but the feeling of peace and happiness you get by serving the Lord will outweigh a pile of money. What's your name, if I might ask?"

"Amy, my name is Amy." She felt a blush spread over her cheeks and a part of her soul sensed an opportunity.

"Amy, I'd consider it a personal favor if you would spend an evening hearing my proposal. Of course, I'll buy dinner. No strings attached."

"Thank you for the compliments, but I don't have any experience working in a revival, particularly with a preacher as gifted as you."

He admired that she played the part well. She lightly touched his arm and her innocent smile came naturally, but underneath he knew there was an exotic soul.

"When do you get off work? You could show me around and then we can drive to Crossville. I need to find a field for the revival. The Lord will guide us in finding one and convincing the owner to rent it for a few nights."

"I get off at four this afternoon, and you can meet me here. I have a change of clothes in my locker in the back. I'd love a nice dinner—the food here is well, you know, routine."

The situation was developing nicely and the preacher knew she could be drawn in. It would not take much persuasion as long as there was money involved.

When he picked her up, Amy looked great and they hit it off with light talk and laughter. A mile north of Crossville there was a typical Carolina shotgun house down the road from a large open field that looked like it would do fine. The preacher pulled into the driveway and a middle-aged woman answered the door and smiled at Amy in the front seat. After a short negotiation with her husband, it was decided the preacher could use the field for his revival. The owner accepted $50.00 for the nights and the deal was sealed with a handshake.

The preacher dropped Amy in front of her apartment downtown, and they agreed to meet for dinner at nine. She was flirty as she closed the door and he smiled, knowing that this was a girl familiar with dealing with men on a financial basis.

*****

For Amy, the ride with the preacher had been exciting and she considered the opportunities. From the moment he walked through the door of the diner, she knew that she'd never seen anyone like him. He was so good looking that he sucked the breath right out of her, paralyzed her, and she was unable to walk the five steps toward him to give him coffee. She was afraid that if she somehow got to him, she would be unable to take the next breath. Of course, she served the coffee, spoke normally, and smiled when he smiled, but inside it took all her conscious power to inhale the next breath and to make sense out of her next word. She hoped he did not notice how she blushed or how she shifted her hips from excitement. This man was someone with more than a little bit of money and plans for upward movement. Amy had been marking time until she could escape this dump. Her schemes hardly ever worked out the first time and so she kept trying, just a bit differently with each try until she got together a plan. With this man, she felt the plan was right. He was a professional and destiny had put them in each other's path. He was a man who could teach her enough to get out of Marsden. She that knew his power was skillfully hidden and felt that there was evil below the surface. She'd rarely known that kind of man, but sensed she could adapt using one of the roles that worked with other men. Acting either dominant or submissive would produce different results, but either of them would be useful in winning him over. She had an opportunity when he picked her up for dinner.

*****

The preacher knew that his plan matched this girl's ambitions. When he picked her up, he would discuss her role at the revival. She had another plan. After the LeBaron's door closed, Amy pulled him close and her fingers gripped the back of his neck as she hissed into his ear, "Make love to me now. I need you."

Each could barely contain themself on the drive, and after the door closed at the Restful Inn, they went right to it. For the next day, the only thing either knew was intertwined bodies and sexual novelty with infrequent bouts of sleep and food. The preacher sensed that Amy's weakness was to believe in love—irresponsible carelessness— the desire to make a fool of oneself with a lover. To his surprise, he matched her intensity in spite of their short time together. In his heart, he knew that of all the girls he'd known, Amy was the one who had the power to make him irrational and could tangle his net.

In the middle of sex, the thought came into his mind that her rosy cheeks were the perfect blend of innocence and sensuality that would draw money from both men and women at the revival. In the afterglow of an athletic session, Amy heard his soft words of love and smiled as a deeper blush colored her cheeks.

*****

After they'd washed off the smell of sex, they passed small talk over dinner and joked that they might be on the way to a meaningful relationship. "Tell me how much money there is in a revival," she purred as she molded against him and whispered into his ear what she could perform back at the Restful Inn. He hated to turn down the offer, but knew he had plenty of time with her. She was in the game until the revival was done.

"There is plenty of money. Plenty for me and plenty for you if you can do the job," and he smiled what he hoped was a smile promising lots of money.

He needed one more staff member and had to make up for lost time spending the afternoon with Amy. She pouted as he dropped her downtown and explained that he had business. She wondered if maybe she'd pushed too hard.

He needed a man to play the preacher's assistant and chances were high that he'd find that man downtown in the bowling alley. Laughter and loud talk covered the noise of the crashing pins as he moved into the dark room and surveyed the cast of characters from the end of the bar. Most of the men and women were drunk, or nearly so, but one scruffy man at the far end of the bar drank quietly, his head down and barely listened to the stories he'd heard before. He was a bum; his boots gave him away, muddy boots worn beyond when they needed reshodding, but his clothes were clean and there were lighter patches of worn material at the knees and elbows.

On the surface, he looked like dull white trash, but beneath he was alert while those around him were drunk. This could be a reliable employee. The preacher took the seat next to him and offered a beer. The man nodded and looked up with his crooked smile.

"What are you doing here, mister; you look like you don't fit, is there something on your mind?"

"I like your attitude; you seem like a man looking for an opportunity."

"Sitting here drinking your beer is not what it looks like; you give me too much credit. I'm just here watching people have a good time. My name is Ham Roosevelt, and yours is?"

"You can call me the preacher. It's better that I don't know your full name—one less way to connect us. I prefer first names or better yet, just initials. There are so many names you could borrow, but Ham suits you. Let's go with that."

*****

When Ham met the preacher that night at the bowling alley, his life gained purpose. He pegged the preacher as a joker, sure enough. That first time they met, the preacher told Ham to his face that he looked like a turd that had oozed into a dirty shirt. The preacher said he'd need to be cleaned up to be worth anything. Ham took that as a job offer, and the preacher outlined the particulars.

Ham admitted that he'd never done the revival con, but added that during his childhood a revival was his first opportunity for petty thievery—wallets left on benches or change under the chairs. The preacher nodded at that story and over the third beer, painted this revival as a no-fail, big return game. Ham would be a partner in the profits, along with a girl the preacher hired. The con was to last two nights to harvest the money and out before anyone was the wiser. The preacher liked Ham's style and thought he could carry the role of his assistant. The assistant would cue the music, introduce the preacher, and help the infirm to the stage when healing was on the schedule. He'd sell merchandise before and after the revival. Ham nodded acceptance and the preacher smiled.

Ham would need a new outfit—one more upscale, with a collared shirt, a dark jacket, and clean black pants—and the preacher would provide all the props.

After the preacher left, Ham reflected on the image from childhood that had defined his life. Chubby fingers were curled around his mother's thumb as she towed him along the sidewalk. People passed and he heard the whispered words *white trash*. Ham asked his mother what that meant. She said the words he's remembered ever since, "It means us, honey...we're white trash." Now, the preacher's offer was an opportunity to move beyond white trash thievery and into serious cash.

Ham's life before the preacher had been low yield but a low risk. He'd managed to avoid a stained soul, except for that one time after midnight, behind a carnival tent in the fog, when he witnessed the murder of a townie by a drunken friend. It had been more frightening because of the shadows, the knife pounding up and down on the crouched body and the silhouette of his friend bending over to take the wallet. During the getaway, the friend ran right by Ham and threw the knife at his feet. Ham went to help the stabbed guy, but he was already dead and images of fresh blood and spilled body fluid mixed with the pungent smell of death often haunted his dreams.

Since the stabbing, Ham kept a low profile and learned to be adaptable to small schemes, but was always on the lookout for an opportunity for easy money. He thought it prophetic that an opportunity found him in this seedy bar—go figure.

The preacher told Ham his first job was to recruit two shills to act as the sick for the healing part of the revival. Men or women, they needed to be able to keep their mouths shut, but had to look sickly or lame or blind or deaf—smooth players with believable afflictions. More than one deformity was a bonus. They would need to meet the preacher that evening for auditions.

Ham found several candidates at the shelter and knew they needed the money. Any scheme would be fine with them under whatever terms were offered, and any money was more than they had now.

Later, Ham's friends showed up behind the bowling alley for the audition. One had a clubfoot, but could walk almost normal if she worked at it. She hung the arm limp at her side and there was a rhythm as she pulled the leg along. Her outfit was vintage shelter wear. The second had a dirty eye patch over a milky right eye and such poor vision out of the other eye that he would fail any eye test. He nodded at the preacher with stained Chiclet teeth and promised to follow directions about what he was supposed to see. The preacher removed the patch and asked the man to show a blank stare and a rolling eye as a blind person would affect. The man was convincing and the preacher told him to wait with the clubfoot woman. The last applicant was a shriveled old man with arthritis who could transform from crippled to standing straight on demand. He wore a long dirty coat to highlight the deformity, even in the summer heat. He swore the transformation worked well for him on street corners for petty cash. The preacher rejected him, but gave him five dollars for his trouble. The other two agreed to be healed on the night of the revival for $25.00 cash, paid after the show.

After the infirm had gone, Amy showed up. From that first moment of meeting her, Ham thought she was a country beauty with sex to spare. The preacher sat both of them down beside the LeBaron and started their lessons. Lesson number one was that a revival gets people's attention. It provides a new voice and new inspiration. New was the operative word because regular churchgoers, although they got the same blabber every Sunday, enjoyed the novelty of a new preacher. Those souls on the fence who might not be able to commit to any one religion used a revival as an opportunity to contact their spiritual side without having to commit. This revival was to go by the name of Goodness Reflected in the Mirror Ministries, a name with a ring to it.

*****

The preacher continued, "We're here to do a con, and it has to be perfectly timed to be successful. Unlike politicians who are elected to take everyone's money, we preachers are privileged and don't require an election."

Ham hardly listened and closed his eyes; the preacher's words were common sense stuff that any grifter knew. Amy watched at full attention, soaking in the practical knowledge. Suddenly, the preacher's open palm shot across the table and slapped Ham's jaw, hard. The speed and accuracy brought to mind a viper, fangs and head forward and striking with no sound. Although Ham pulled his head back a bit when the air stirred, it was not enough to avoid the slap. In addition to being silent and deadly accurate, the slap drove home the importance of focusing on the preacher's every word. Ham learned then that the preacher was a man of few words, but many communications. As the sting on his cheek burned, he felt a need to rebel, a need to punish the preacher for embarrassing him in front of Amy. Ham held a grudge and the slap created a black mark on his invisible tally sheet for some kind of revenge on the preacher yet to come. Before the sound of the slap had passed, the preacher looked at Ham, eyes boring into his eyes, and sighed.

"Hmmm." The inflection covered the meat of the matter for an observant person. "Do you know enough to daydream white trash? This is prime stuff I'm teaching you, and it requires your complete attention. Every move must be finely tuned, and I'm telling you the way I want it. Anyone who daydreams endangers us all, so listen up."

The three of them spent the rest of the evening supervising roadies setting the tent, placing bug screens along the flaps, and arranging chairs in a semicircle around the stage. The stage was elevated six inches off the floor so the preacher could jump into the audience when needed. The same light blue bunting trimmed the stage and the doorways. Bare bulbs were strung on wire hung from the ceiling to give a sense of spiritual darkness that tapered into the tent peak. They tested the placement in the darkened tent to get it right. Amy and the preacher left together, and as they left, the preacher's arm slipped around Amy's waist and patted her ass. Ham tried to look away but could not, as his eyes were watching that same ass.

Early the next morning, Ham was assigned to cut and fold three-by-three-inch black cotton prayer clothes and seal them in envelopes. Amy filled bottles with blessed water—or really, cloudy water. The preacher said impurities implied stronger healing power. Luckily, Marsden's water looked cloudy out of the tap and was free. Every bottle needed a cork so that the person could pull a drop or two when needed to help heal some life affliction. The final item to be offered was a small sealed envelope labeled "PRAYER POWER" and a red stamp beneath that read "DO NOT OPEN." Inside was a plain white business card with the printed words "God's grace is with you" in case the believer mistakenly opened it. Each item was priced at five dollars; an amount that the preacher said was enough to make the purchase dear but not out of the reach of any of the faithful. The prayer clothes, blessed water bottles, and prayer power envelopes were stacked in boxes behind the stage. The preacher figured about 250 of each should be enough for the two days, but only fifty prayer cloths would be put out the first night to suggest they might be in limited supply. Blessed water and prayer power envelopes would be added the second night to encourage people to buy them as a set, priced at $14.00. At the last minute, the preacher decided to add fifty more of each. The props were in place.

The preacher stressed that an important quality of a revival was that the tent was clean and the chairs arranged in orderly rows. In the afternoon, Ham worked in the hot humid tent to get everything like the preacher wanted. The heat nearly made him pass out and his sweat mixed with grass and bugs; it was a dirty job. Amy and the preacher were off somewhere and Ham thought it was probably somewhere cool. It was obvious that there was something happening between them and Ham wanted some of that action. When the two of them showed up later, Amy looked ridden hard with the lingering smell of sex drifting behind her into the tent. She fanned herself, and to oblige, the preacher told a roadie to bring a fan to blow around the hot air. After fifteen minutes, they left with more orders for Ham to finish up.

All the planning came together that night. Ham wore dark wool pants with a heavy woolen jacket, and his beige shirt was soaked with sweat. The preacher told him those were the only clothes available in his size at the shelter. As a consolation, the preacher let him stand in front of a fan until the show started. In contrast, the preacher's outfit looked cool and comfortable. He was wearing a lightweight gray coat, slacks, brown boots, and a pale blue shirt. There was a heavy wooden cross around his neck, and his black hair was swept back and lightly oiled. His teeth sparkled as he smiled at Ham's discomfort and he slipped his arm around Amy's waist.

Amy had on a modest knee-length blue cotton dress, the kind that rode up considerably on her legs when she bent down to assist one of the faithful. The top hugged her breasts, not tight enough to offend the ladies, but firm enough for the men to notice. She wore white ankle socks that accentuated her perfect legs and shiny Mary Janes. Her blonde hair was dyed a mousy brown and pulled into a ponytail. No doubt about it, the girl was the picture of subtle sexual energy in a package of innocence. Ham admitted to himself that he'd only met a few girls like her, but each of them had been a rare and addictive treasure. He started to hope there might be a chance to sample Amy's talents after the preacher left town. He watched Amy and the preacher standing beside each other as both of them looked into each other's eyes; her eyes shone with love, his with the excitement of the deception. Ham looked away. Amy had fallen for the preacher, fallen hard, and his chances with her were fading. To cover all bases, Amy looked at Ham and smiled…an invitation…then blinked hard to make her eyes glossy bright for the show. She was ready.

The plan was for two hours of preaching on the first night and a shorter preaching session, then thirty minutes of healing on the last night. Amy and Ham would collect donations throughout the service. The preacher let them know that he would be watching the cash, so it all needed to come backstage with no shortages.

*****

Music started at 7:00 pm, just loud enough to draw attention to the lighted tent entrance in the darkening field. Ham borrowed a tape player and used the preacher's music. When they needed the faithful to sing along, he'd crank up the volume. They used familiar revival songs as the draw. The faithful, country people by their outfits, slowly moved into the tent, and Amy seated them with the most reverent-looking toward the front and doubters toward the back. Men sat quietly and women gently fanned the hot air, smiled, and whispered to friends. Each night, aisle seats were reserved for the infirm shills. Items for sale were out of sight behind the stage. Everyone was seated by eight o'clock, and the tent flap closed. The preacher looked out from behind the stage at the few empty seats in the front row and smiled. Ham played singin' music that everyone knew: the classic "Shout to the Lord" and a group of Windell Capel classics, "The Devil's on the Phone Dialing 9-1-1" and "How Far is Heaven." Amy and Ham sang as loud as they could from the back and the crowd joined them and clapped in time. After Windell's music warmed everyone, Ham moved to the side of the stage and started the introduction with the words, pauses, and inflections the preacher gave him.

"Please welcome to our community a man called by God, a man with the gift of speech to bring God's word to all people, a man who will touch each of us tonight. He's a powerful man who will heal through God's touch, healing as you've never seen from a doctor. Please open your hearts to his words and be saved. Please welcome the preacher." Polite applause erupted from the audience as the preacher bounded onto the stage.

At the front edge, he bowed his head and started with a prayer, as if speaking grace to friends at a dinner table. "Let us ask God to enlighten us, to open our minds...so that tonight, through our ministry of Goodness Reflected in the Mirror, we can see the mirror of our soul. At birth, God gave each of us a perfect soul, untarnished by the sins of the world. As we've lived our life, the mirror of our soul has become cloudy, tarnished by our lifetime of sin. Let us pray that during this revival we can wipe away the grime and restore the bright soul of our birth. Pray with me that over the next two nights we may see ourselves clearly, that we may recognize our special beauty, and that through prayer we can wipe our mirror clean of sin. I assure you that if you let yourselves be guided by my words, the mirror of your soul will be cleansed. Can I get an amen?" Each phrase was emphasized by his nods toward the crowd as he scanned from right to left to include them all in his message. The crowd warmed as Amy and Ham led the applause.

He moved to the middle of the stage and in his softest voice, the preacher asked the audience to close their eyes. "Raise your hand if you can see Heaven." No one raised a hand, and he nodded. "Open your eyes and see that your brothers and sisters have not seen Heaven. I tell you that our minds are limited, that only a prophet can see Heaven…that God blocks our vision of eternal glory and makes Heaven too far away for us to see. He demands faith. Through his ministers, God walks among us, giving us hope that even if we can't see eternal glory, we have faith that it's there." His left hand swung wide across the audience, including them in the vision.

"If you follow the path I'll show you tonight, you can rest in glory at the end of your days. Love your brothers my friends…if we follow that simple formula, everyone here tonight, even the most sinful, can gain salvation. To love our brothers requires us to look after the sick and the weak and the infirm, and the ministers of the cloth who guide them." His body glided across the stage, alert and graceful, as he glanced at the audience to assure they were caught up in his words. When he talked of Heaven, his hands extended in a cross, inviting the audience, all of them, to join in the vision he painted.

His audience of sheep nodded as one head. As if confiding a secret, the preacher bent low and addressed the front rows. He whispered that he knew from God what love was about, and what it needed to be. His voice changed, and he shouted to the audience that he wouldn't tell them any lies; he'd seen paradise, but only in a dream, and only for a second. "God spoke to me, and it was the most musical, soothing voice. God spoke only one word and my soul was lifted. The word will be imprinted on my brain till the day I die— love, my brothers and sisters, the word was love." His right hand tapped his heart as he paused to let the word echo inside the tent, and the air was still, everyone waiting for his next revelation.

To break the silence, he transitioned in the space of two breaths from the soothing voice of love to shouting from the stage, shouts punctuated by thin streams of spittle coming out of his mouth and his right hand pumping up and down with each word as if puncturing an invisible cluster of balloons in the peak of the tent. Hell was real and some in the audience would burn in that terrible state for all eternity. The crowd came alive with his description of the fires of

Hell and some jumped to their feet and hid their faces in fear. The preacher's body changed and became fierce and defensive of his new flock as he stood in the center of the stage, gripping the back of the chair with both hands. The audience believed he was standing off the minions of Hell. He preached fire, that only by working every waking hour for the salvation of their brothers could they avoid burning in Hell for eternity. In the south, in the summer, the crowd felt the heat around them in that tent and he made the heat but a tiny measure of how the fire of Hell would feel—no mention of the smell of brimstone was needed. From the back, Ham was moved to shout for all of them to be saved from the fires of Hell and momentarily forgot that he was part of the deception. Across the tent, Amy looked angelic, nodding and smiling as if she and Ham were already walking hand in hand on the road to Heaven.

From the back of the tent, on cue Ham shouted, "Ain't it the truth, Preacher," and raised his right hand in testimony, moving it back and forth like a pendulum of faith. Amy swayed in rhythm to the soft music on the other side of tent, the rhythm of her hips marked by the movement of her ponytail. In that moment, Ham, and even Amy, believed that the preacher could convince the people in that tent that evil could be good, that their sins were a necessary pathway to salvation. The preacher's words moved Ham so that his shouts of joy and praise were almost genuine. The crowd murmured in agreement, nodding and slowly waving their arms back and forth as if possessed, their nods corresponding with each punctuated word—it mattered not whether the preacher spoke of Heaven or Hell—the audience embraced the image. The preacher paused after about an hour and cued Ham to start another round of music. At the edge of the stage, he looked at the audience and smiled, willing them to believe he'd given them his all and that he needed to recharge before giving them more inspiration. In a flourish, the preacher wiped sweat from his brow and disappeared behind the stage. Ham and Amy passed baskets and Amy bent low to reach the middle of each aisle. Men's heads turned to appreciate her white thigh while their women fanned and dropped their money into the basket. Ham only needed to smile and nod to each person, silently coaxing them to donate all they could. The energy and visions of the preacher's words had passed, and Ham and Amy got back to their jobs.

After the intermission, there were more songs, old-fashioned preaching with seizure movement and fainting, then a big finish when the preacher painted a verbal picture of Heaven. His words made the glory of Heaven vivid in the minds of each person in the audience. People saw the images he painted as if in a movie and they wanted to be there with their wife, their family, and with all their brothers and sisters. Amy and Ham passed the basket, and more folding money filled it.

The preacher told the audience about the prayer cloths for sale outside the tent and guaranteed the power of the cloth to heal body and soul. He crooned that the cloth, wiped gently over any part of the body afflicted with illness, would restore health by driving out the demon that caused the illness. He cautioned that the cloth was never to be washed and would stop being effective if used too often, so it might be prudent to buy more than one. Sales were brisk.

His final words for the night spoke to them about a stone thrown into still water, about ripples radiating outward toward the shore. He jumped off the stage, paced along the front rows, and implored each member of the audience to become those ripples and to bring their friends the following night to witness love and salvation. In his softest voice, he made them believe that the healing power of God, the ripple that started with each of them, could spread to all the worthy people in Crossville. There was not the faintest movement of air in the tent as he finished and people waited for him to show them more images of salvation before they took their next breath. Every mouth sighed disappointment that their glimpse of Heaven had ended for the night.

After the crowd left, the three team members gathered for a debriefing. The night had gone well according to the preacher, and he was pleased with how Ham's and Amy's performance infused the crowd. He scooped up the bag of cash and drove back to Marsden in the LeBaron, dropping Ham at a cheap hotel on the outskirts. He gave Ham ten dollars for essentials and said he would have a different set of clothes for the next night. After supper at the Waffle House, there was still five dollars left. Lying on the sway-backed mattress, stripped down to underwear, the cool breeze felt heavenly blowing over Ham. He recalled just one image from the con: an elderly couple in rapture over the preacher's words, the woman dropping $20.00 in the basket and afterward buying four prayer clothes for $19.00. He wondered where the money had come from and if they would miss it. As sleep came, Ham's mother's words crept across his memory. "There's surely a special place in Hell for those who steal from the religious."

*****

The next day passed uneventfully. The preacher picked up the infirm from the shelter in Marsden and brought them to the motel where Ham rehearsed their role. After a few practices, there was nothing for them to do but watch TV and eat takeout from the Waffle House. The clubfoot woman entertained them with her hundred jokes, most of them about religion.

At dusk, the crowd had doubled—friends called friends to witness and be saved and the soft music enticed them into the tent. There were rows of the faithful filling the chairs and even more standing around the sides. Amy seated their two shills on the aisles on either side, but seated any genuine infirm close to the middle of a row.

Ham wore a light-colored woolen coat, dark pants, a blue cotton shirt, and a black string tie. Amy had changed to a long multicolored skirt and a pale white top that was tight, as if it had come as a hand-me-down from an older sister. The blouse gapped at each button to highlight her figure and allow glimpses of her white bra for any of the men who might look. She wore dark eye makeup to create a mysterious look, transformed in one night from an innocent girl to a girl possessed by the power of the Lord. She looked at Ham and licked her lips and he saw a different image of Heaven.

The preacher looked apostolic in a cool blue seersucker suit, pale yellow cotton shirt, and the heavy wooden cross around his neck. His smile was electric, and his teeth sparkled. At the tent entrance, he looked each man in the eye as he pumped his hand and substituted a light touch on the forearm for each woman. He smiled at young girls to make them want to be drawn into conversation with him. As he looked into each person's eyes, especially a woman's eyes, he spoke soft words in a persuasive voice. His voice attracted the crowd like a magnet pulling iron filings. After Ham's introduction, the preacher moved on stage gracefully, looked out at the audience, pointed at some, and smiled at all.

Tonight, he picked up the theme he'd left the previous night and started in a soft voice using words that caressed the glowing image of redemption. His image of Heaven was clear and beautiful, a melody familiar to each person, but with clearer notes. He told the faithful that the word *revive* meant to live again, to revive a life that had almost expired, to rekindle a flame that was nearly extinguished from a vital spark. He preached that none of them would think of reviving nature—the midday sun or the ocean or the rushing river when it overflowed its banks—that it's only man who needed reviving. He paced the semicircle of the stage and his hands drew images of the sun or the rushing river. From his opening words, the crowd was transformed into brothers and sisters infused with faith, anxious to accept everything he told them. He painted colorful images of love, of families, and of salvation culminating in a multicolored vision of the eternal glory waiting for each of them. Rapture was within their grasp if they heeded his words and regularly used the prayer tools available at the meeting. Only with his help and a strong belief could they hope to wipe away their lifetime of sin. Unlike other preachers, his pitch was delivered with eye contact to each member of the audience and that made it personal and so believable.

Then silence, a pause long enough for ten breaths, before his posture changed and he paced the stage as a creature possessed. He embodied a man in Hell, writhing and shaking for the benefit of all believers. Vivid images of burning and hopelessness swirled through the crowd, and the lights dimmed, flickered, and came bright again as if the devil was walking in the room and the preacher was ready to do battle with him. The songs Ham played sung stern warnings of the perils of a private hell for each person and he was touched by the preacher's words of Heaven and feared his vision of Hell—the performance swayed Ham's emotions and those of the audience back and forth from Heaven to Hell and back again. The preacher's body language and powerful voice amplified the eternal contrasts and each member of the audience saw images of Hell as if projected from the cinema. It was a con, but nonetheless Ham felt a need to look into the mirror of his soul and be cleansed.

As a buildup to the healing, the preacher used an energy trick he'd learned from a revival preacher on the circuit. He asked the faithful to raise their hands, close their eyes, and concentrate their spiritual energy. The audience obliged with a hundred faces looking to the top of the tent and concentrating on God's grace. It was a virtuoso performance. Ham recalled that at a revival as a child he'd tried the concentration trick, but never felt anything until tonight. Tonight he felt the grace of God and he had to concentrate to pass the basket.

Amy seemed enraptured as she bent to reach the middle seats and lightly brushed her breast against the legs of the men sitting on the aisle. This energy channel propelled the hands of the faithful to drop their folding money into the basket.

After another round of songs, Ham introduced the next act. "Friends, we have listened, we have been uplifted, and we have channeled God's grace into our hearts. The power of our prayers has enabled the preacher to concentrate his healing power. He will now heal those unfortunate souls among us who have come tonight wearing their faith like a bright badge hoping to be made whole again."

The preacher walked onto the stage with his head bowed and shoulders slumped as if wearing the heavy mantle of responsibility. He paused and looked at the crowd with tears in his eyes. "Being a preacher can be discouraging, but there are moments of profound joy. As I looked at your donations last night, I was encouraged that you have allowed our mission to continue, and I thank you. Tonight I encourage you to give what you can so that our mission may not just continue, but can move forward to reach other cities. Preaching is often sad, sad work, and it's painful when my words are ignored. Last night you showed me that your ears are not deaf, and that your mind is open to the power of God. Those who have come tonight as new visitors, we welcome you. Those who have returned from last night, I give a new challenge: to allow your soul to be filled to the brim with the grace of God.

As a special offering tonight, we have bottles of blessed water and envelopes filled with prayer power. I encourage you to take home the prayer cloth to clean your mirror, to take home the healing water to lift your soul above disease, and to use the prayer envelope to guide your worship.

Take one, take two, or take more in order to reap the maximum benefit. Take one of each for your friends who could not be here so that they may experience the revival of their soul.

Most of you are healthy, and your eyes are bright, but some of you here tonight do not have those advantages. For the infirm that have come tonight hoping for a chance at health and redemption, we welcome you—no matter your affliction. Health and redemption are one side of a coin, and disease and damnation are the dark side of that coin. On the bright side of the coin is the faith the infirm bring tonight, hoping for God's healing grace to renew their bodies. Tonight, all of us are alive, but some among you live with the challenges God has given you. Brothers and sisters, we must love our friends who suffer with disease and channel our energy to revive their souls. By reviving their souls, their bodies will be made whole. No matter how sinful, there's a spiritual life in each of us, our mirror that can be cleansed, and our soul that can be revived."

Shouts of "Love our brothers" rang through the tent and Ham cued the music. The songs echoed the preacher's message with "A Shelter in the Time of Storm" and "On Jordan's Stormy Banks." The preacher stood immobile at the center of the stage, head bowed, and hands limp at his side, swaying to his own rhythm, gathering strength. The audience took up that same rhythm while Amy and Ham sang, swayed, and raised their hands. The tent became a moving organism with a heart beating in unison. For all in the audience, a healing at a revival was an event that demanded attention. To witness a healing, to see something so fantasmical, prompted a woman in the audience to whisper that they were to witness with their own eyes that Jesus walked among them.

The preacher looked over the audience, eyes scanning for his infirm, before pointing to the blind man with the dirty eye patch on the aisle. The man stood with the help of those around him and Amy helped him to the stage. He navigated the step at the front of the stage and then turned to look at the audience. His roving eye and his slack shoulders signaled that he had been defeated by disease. Ham knew that under his defeated look was a keen alertness, and the man played the part with the skill of any performer. The preacher beckoned, and the man ambled across the stage with his head low and bobbing like a cow following the herd.

"What is your name brother?" In return, he received guttural sounds that might be a name. The preacher removed the dirty eye patch, and those men and women in the front rows gasped at the cloudy white eye socket.

"How long have you been blind my son?" The man shrugged. "How many fingers do you see?" The man shrugged again, and the roving eye ran over the audience.

The preacher moved in front of the blind man and held a prayer cloth over his eyes while mumbling indistinguishable words. After a suitable time of suspense, the preacher removed the cloth. The man turned to look at the audience as if awakened. His good eye had stopped roving, and he smiled a crooked smile. The preacher asked him to count the fingers as he held the same three fingers in front of his jacket, and the man lifted three fingers.

The preacher smiled and shouted "Thank you God! Believe my brother, and use this prayer cloth every morning to make your eyesight even better." Gasps of wonder arose from the audience and those in the front row whispered from row to row about the large tear at the corner of the man's good eye as he took the prayer cloth and walked off stage, his head held high. As he passed, men and women along the aisle held handkerchiefs to their faces in amazement.

No one noticed when the man left the tent because as soon as he'd left the stage, the preacher swayed as if he had used all of his energy in the healing and fell into the chair with both hands holding tight to the seat.

As one voice, the audience cried out, shocked and awed, and several left their seats to attend to the preacher.

Ham knew his cue and blocked the stage, while clapping and shouting "Praise the Lord" and looking to the top of the tent. His actions were taken up by the audience and every one of the faithful raised their hands and shouted praise for the preacher. There was a basket on the front edge of the stage for contributions and people came forward. The preacher remained center stage with his head bowed and eyes closed to gather his strength for what was to follow.

After minutes passed and low background music stopped, the preacher moved to the side of his chair and rubbed his head with a prayer cloth to gather strength. After more seconds, he turned to the audience, imploring them to shout to God to give him strength. On demand, shouts went up from around the tent, different words and different voices, but all loud and directed toward the peak of the tent. Gradually, the preacher's breathing slowed and deepened and he swayed once more before lifting his head to show the audience that through their intervention he had become a man recharged by God's grace. Every eye of the flock saw their own image of the holy man and silently wished him to heal their soul. From the stage, it resembled a tableau of still life.

The preacher stood, his shoulders again bowed by the weighty mantle of healing, and asked Ham to select someone from the audience with a bone disease. Ham scanned the audience and pointed to the woman with the clubfoot. She raised her crooked hand in joy as if she'd just been selected as a game show contestant. Amy helped her stand and supported her to the stage as she pulled her bad foot behind and hung her right arm loosely at her side. A pitiful sight for the audience;

114

the image enhanced by tattered clothes. With Amy's help, the woman ascended and stood on the edge of the stage with her eyes focused on the preacher. He took her left hand and together they moved across the stage in painfully slow movements. The audience hung on every step, fearful that she might fall. The preacher asked her to sit in his chair in the center of the stage.

"God has heard your prayers, sister. What is your wish?"

"I ask God to give me back the use of my arm, preacher. It has been weak since a stroke five years ago and I can't make do with just my left arm."

"Do you believe?"

"Yes, Preacher, I believe in the power of God, in his power to heal my soul and his power to wipe the mirror of my soul clean of sin, just like you've told us the last two nights. I confess that I've been a sinner, sometimes sinned so bad that I can't bear to talk of it. I want my soul to be new again, clean, and bright. I know that if you can cleanse my soul, my arm will work again. I have faith that you can work a miracle, even on a sinner like me." Hearing all that story, Ham thought she might have overplayed the part from what they'd rehearsed, but the preacher was unfazed.

"Pray with me, sister, and I ask the faithful to send their prayers to the stage so that your soul can be wiped clean of sin." He circled to the back of her chair and pulled a bottle of blessed water from his coat. In an instant, he sprinkled a few drops on a prayer cloth, mumbling words of faith into the cloth. He gently rubbed the cloth along her arm, starting at her shoulder and finishing at the tips of her fingers. He repeated the action once, twice, and yet again before resting his hands on her shoulders. He closed his eyes and mumbled soft words, then paused, bowed, and touched the back of her head with his forehead. The timing was brilliant, just long enough for magic to happen, but not long enough for the audience to lose focus.

He slowly walked around to the front of the women and shouted into the darkness at the top of the tent, "Demons, evil hitchhikers, be gone from this woman's arm. Sister, stand for me now and feel the grace of God."

She stood and tentatively moved her arm, stiff at first, then up and down as mobile and limber as any member of the audience. The audience gasped as she moved to embrace the preacher with both arms. She cried loud sobs into the preacher's shoulder, and on cue, the audience delivered cries and shouts of "Praise the Lord." This time the shouts of praise were spontaneous and Amy and Ham marveled at his magic.

"Go, sister, and love your neighbors. Use the prayer cloth and the blessed waters and your right arm will become stronger." As she left the stage, she moved her arm in a circle as a show, and her dragging clubfoot seemed less important. Neighbors gently touched her arm to garner some of the power as she passed down the aisle. She smiled at each of them. Ham made a note to commend her on the performance and to ask the preacher to give her an extra few dollars.

The preacher swayed again, his energy sapped by the healing, and the audience cried out again, afraid that the healing had been too taxing. He stumbled back to his chair and sat, exhausted, his head bowed and his hands on his forehead. Amy ran from the back, waving a five-dollar bill. She cried genuine tears as she shouted to the audience that the money was from the woman—all that she could afford, but worth it for the use of her arm. More than half of the audience approached the stage with their folded money and raised their arms toward the resting preacher as they dropped bills into the basket. Ham played soft music and those in the crowd who had given all their money swayed in their seats and hummed softly as they raised their hands in thanks.

As a finale, the preacher used a special chemical mixture that turned blood red with sweat. Before the show, he had applied it to his forehead in the shape of a cross. As the heat in the tent increased and the audience's fervor over the healings built, the mixture turned blood red with the preacher's sweat and dripped thin rivulets down his forehead. Whispers started in the front row and spread in waves through the audience. Shouts of wonder rang through the tent.

Ham yelled from the back. "Surely this is a sign from God. The preacher suffers because he has cast out the devils from those unfortunates." As if the bleeding were a necessary burden of healing, the preacher dabbed his forehead with the special prayer cloth, but the dripping continued, now radiating out from the original cross. He'd practiced enough to know that after five wipes with the rag, the chemical solution would turn clear, and he could wipe his forehead clean. After the last wipe, he handed the prayer cloth soaked with his sweat to an old woman in the front row. She nearly fainted with the gift and pressed it to her mouth. The audience marveled that no red color appeared on her mouth or on the cloth.

After that spectacle there was no need to pass the basket, the crowd rushed the stage to touch the cloth and to deposit their money as they pushed toward the preacher. Amy walked to his side to shield him and Ham rushed the stage, a broom held in a military pose, as if to sweep away any remaining demons and hold back the crowd.

After the commotion settled, Ham's cue was to thank the crowd for coming and to speak for the preacher who sat center stage, too exhausted to speak another word. "Friends, brothers and sisters, you have witnessed miracles tonight, your soul has been touched and the demons of disease have been vanquished. You've seen for yourself how holy items force demons to retreat in fear.

You have it in your power to take those items home and use them for yourself, for your family, and for all sinners to help them cleanse their souls. As you leave tonight, pray for the preacher that he may regain his power to help others. Go with God."

The faithful filed out of the tent and more than a few looked back at the preacher sitting quietly on stage and women murmured prayers for his welfare. Amy and Ham guided them out the door and watched the lights from the last car drive out of the field. She looked at Ham, tired after two nights of being good and flashed him a look of ready-to-do-evil that made him believe the look was for him. Both felt that what evil they had done escaped the tent and was safely diffusing into the night air. Any rogue religious beliefs that had been awakened by the preacher also diffused into the air and all that was left was a sticky southern night. They smiled at the success of the con. Amy went to find the preacher while Ham reflected on his feelings. The con was finished and for those two nights, his morality had blown around the tent like a fart that no one admits. This was just a job, but a job with consequences he'd puzzle over for years to come. The preacher dredged up those long-forgotten childhood perceptions of Heaven, Hell, and an afterlife and Ham wasn't sure what to do about the emotions. On the plus side, there was money due for a job well done. The preacher had his sack of cash, and Ham expected the preacher would pay him a good percentage. In the bar, the preacher promised that Ham would be a partner, but he never gave details on how much money that might mean. In Ham's mind, whatever the preacher paid, it wouldn't be enough. It was the time to act.

It was just the two of them outside the tent and in the light of the quarter moon, they were shadows. The preacher smiled and held out his hand, passing across a roll of bills. It was too dark to tell denominations, but Ham guessed at somewhere around one hundred dollars. Ham grinned as he pocketed the cash and held out his hand. In the pale moonlight, off stage and without props, the preacher was a department store manikin with a pasted grin and a sweaty palm. Ham was not any better. The smiles between the two men were too much; the way someone smiles when they can't stand somebody. The preacher must have known how much Ham hated him for duping those people, hated him for using Amy for his pleasure, and most of all hated him for taking all that money for himself. It ran through Ham's mind about his revenge for the preacher planning every slight to make Ham look like a bumpkin in front of Amy. The time for revenge had come. Ham planned to take all the money, the car and Amy and leave with a head start. The preacher would have to walk back to Marsden. It was just the two of them in the field, looking daggers at each other, a roll of bills for one and a bag of cash for the other. Ham pulled the knife from his shirt and shook it at the preacher. The long blade reflected in the moonlight.

The preacher's smile never wavered. "You haven't changed since I picked you out of that bar. You're white trash and white trash is all you'll ever be. Go back to your small town bowling alley, back to sipping beer and waiting for some petty opportunity, but you'll never find a con as good as this one. At first, I thought there was hope for you. You did a good job. I was going to offer you some work down the line, but not now. I never forget when someone crosses me."

A small black semi automatic appeared from the preacher's coat pocket and he ordered Ham to drop the knife.

"If I see you again, I'll empty this pistol into your head. Now get out of here."

*****

The preacher turned his back, knowing Ham was no longer a threat. If you knocked a man down enough, he learned not to get up. The one hundred dollars was enough; Ham had earned it. The preacher had expected the double cross. When you worked the con, there was at least one surprise, and being prepared was what made the preacher a professional. That poor goof would have a long dark walk back to town, and he might be back in Marsden by morning if someone picked him up. He was out of the picture.

Amy had agreed to wait in the car while the preacher did his business with Ham. She was proving to be an excellent associate, anticipating what he needed, acting the part, and most importantly, providing enthusiastic sex on demand. She was waiting in the front seat and even in the dim moonlight, she looked outstanding. On the drive back to the Starlight, she stayed close and could not keep her hands off him; even wanted to stop midway in a dark field to get the party started, but the preacher had never liked outdoor sex.

*****

In the room, she popped an iced champagne bottle she'd ordered from the motel management and they toasted success. The preacher poured on the praise and told her with his most sincere smile that it was hard being good with a woman like her, that being bad felt so right—lines he'd always wanted to use. For her part, she knew what he liked and started stripping while softly singing a revival song Ham had played one night. The preacher didn't remember the words, but it seemed like "hell" was in there somewhere. Amy had a great voice, but never got to finish the song. Sex was not like the first time, but then it never was. Her gift was novelty, and she outdid herself.

Afterward, they sipped champagne with the light of the closed blinds just bright enough to see each other's face. Amy turned on her side and thanked him for what he'd taught her. He smiled and told her about Ham and his knife. She did not seem surprised. The preacher pumped it up a bit by telling her that in the few days we'd worked together, he'd grown to hate Ham like poison but feigned a civility to avoid conflict and to see the job through. He stressed that the mark of a professional in any field was to work well with someone you hated. Amy laughed at his cleverness in giving Ham a woolen suit in the middle of summer and making a point of feeling her whenever he got the chance in order to mark his property.

The rest of the night was exhausting. The preacher went into the bathroom around three and wrote a love note on the mirror for Amy to see when she got up. He'd always wanted be that romantic, like in the movies. For him it was an expression of love—the truth and nothing but the truth…but not the whole truth. How easy it was to manipulate the lovesick.

His made it a practice to have wake-up sex with Amy and after a successful con, everything felt more alive. They talked about their future as they cuddled together in the afterglow and early morning sunlight filtered through the drapes. Amy rolled onto her back and whispered, "I think we're something special."

The preacher slipped out of bed and whispered over his shoulder, too low to hear, "we were." As he closed the bathroom door, she never saw him mouth the rest of the thought, "and now we're not."

On the other side of the door, he knew the time had come to dissolve their partnership. He took the small bottle from behind the shelf and looked carefully at the twist top for a full minute… then thirty more seconds, then twenty, then ten, and finally made his decision. Amy called through the door, "Are you all right?"

"Yes, I'm fine. I'll be right out."

He soaked a prayer cloth with the clear liquid, thinking that it would be a short time and a minor struggle before the anesthetic took effect. He held his breath and opened the door. She was lying on her side and breathing softly. After it was done, she would rest peacefully for an hour, and he would be gone in any of four directions.

*****

On her side of the bed, she replayed the revival. Her plan to meet the sheriff outside the tent had gone well and now she just had to wait for events to happen. Meeting the sheriff had gone as planned and Amy provided the preacher's address and room number at the Starlight. She didn't need much time to renew that old acquaintance, because the back seat of the sheriff's car was familiar territory. She'd rendered services there many times before. Last night, as she'd climbed out, he called her a heartless bitch, and she snapped back that he was a horny bastard. It was nothing but sass, but she delivered it with a respect due an officer of the law. She was used to giving sass and even more used to not having any replies. The sheriff had nothing to say, because both statements were as true as they could be.

*****

As the bathroom door opened, there was a loud knock on the outer door, and then a deep voice carried through the door. "Preacher, I know you're in there. We need to talk. Open the door, and we can do this peacefully."

It was all the preacher could do to toss the soaked rag into the bathroom and close the door. He and Amy looked at each other, and she seemed as bewildered as he did. Outside, the sheriff was waiting in the sunshine with his hand on his sidearm. The man's face was etched with deep gray worry lines, wavy and contoured—he was a man used to hearing stories. If someone looked carefully, his mouth laughed, but his eyes were either empty or hooded like the fire had gone or he was hiding his thoughts.

"Yes, Officer, what can I do for you?"

"I'm the sheriff, son, and I've tracked you down to ask about some suspicious activity at your revival last night. An elderly couple says they were robbed after the revival. I thought you might know something that might help identify the thief."

"Robbery? I don't know anything about any robbery. The revival was peaceful, and when I left there was no one around."

"That's not the story I heard. One of our senior citizens and his wife called the office about eleven last night to report the robbery. My deputy drove out to investigate and found an old couple in the field, and she was crying. They said they'd stayed on a bit to talk with you and get some special help with her sister's cancer. The man said a tall thin man approached them in a baggy wool suit, threatened them with a knife, and demanded their money. They didn't want any trouble, so they gave him all they had—$100.00. They swear it happened in the darkness behind the tent after everyone was gone. The woman was shocked because she believed that a revival was one of the safest places in the county. After they gave him the money, the man ducked under the tent flap and disappeared. They were afraid to go after him and it took them a while to get to a phone. The poor woman was too shaken to come to the station, but they promised to come in today to finish the report.

The preacher was puzzled; the description fit Ham, but he'd left Ham outside the tent and there were no cars in the field. Ham was to arrange breaking down the tent in the morning and claimed he had friends coming to pick him up last night. That was his story before the knife incident, so there was no telling what happened after he'd counted the one hundred dollar roll. The preacher knew enough that he could not show doubt in any part of his story; this cop could sense lying through his skin like a snake.

"Sheriff, I've got about a hundred witnesses that I was inside preaching and healing, and my associate, Amy, was with me until this morning and can vouch for me. Isn't that right, Amy?"

"That's true, Sheriff. I was with him, and he didn't rob anybody. I know that a good man is hard to find and this man is innocent. He is a fine man, finer than any I've met."

The sheriff nodded. "Maybe that's true little lady, but we still need to ask him to come to the station to answer some questions and to meet the couple. I'm sure we can clear this up quickly. Now, mister, that's the nice language, if you decide you want a different course, we can bring you down in a less civil way. It's your choice.

"Can I meet you at the station since you haven't told me I'm a suspect?"

"No, I'd prefer you come with me in the car so that we can be sure you make it safely. This young lady can drive down in a few hours to pick you up and if everything checks out, you can be on your way."

Amy looked up and nodded. The preacher finished dressing, handed her the keys, and whispered that he'd be waiting and they would move on together.

She glanced between the sheriff and the preacher as she talked about how he was a gifted healer and made several people whole again at the revival.

She added that they were due to start a revival in South Carolina the next night and needed to be on their way.

"I understand that you have business to attend to, honey. Everybody has business, but this is the law, and the law has to be above any business, even one as blessed as a revival. I'm sure we can resolve this in plenty of time for you both to be on your way."

The sheriff motioned toward the door, and as the preacher left, he looked at Amy and in the same smooth voice he'd used in the revival whispered: "I'll see you at the station in two hours, and we can be together." Amy whispered in reply, "We are soul mates, destined to be together. I will be there." She nodded as the door closed.

On the short drive to the station, the preacher thought new thoughts, evil thoughts, about Ham. The sheriff offered him a seat next to his desk. "Well, mister, I'm going to ask you some routine questions. I'm sure you understand. Can I see some identification please? I hate to keep calling you the preacher when you've got a name."

The preacher handed over his driver's license listing him as Jimmy DeVane with an address in Alexandria, Virginia. "Thank you, Mr. DeVane. I'm sure we can straighten this business out in a few hours, and you can be on your way.

"Start by telling me how you happened to come to Crossville? Tell me about the revival and be as detailed as you can. Walter, set up that recorder so we don't miss any of Mr. DeVane's story." Jimmy told a clean story while the sheriff took some notes and then leaned back in his chair to think it all over. After a pause, he turned to his deputy. "Walter, can you take Mr. DeVane to the back and put him in our best cell until we can sort this out a little better. That couple should be down shortly and we can get their story and ask them to give a description of the robber. Maybe Mr. DeVane will recognize him from the description."

*****

Amy was impressed that the sheriff had come just in time and perfectly retold the story of the elderly couple. Too bad she'd never see him or the back seat of his car again. The description of Ham would start them looking for him. Amy was sure the couple disappeared with their fifty and Ham had probably already left town, so all the loose ends were tied up. She smiled as she cracked the bathroom door and smelled the potent fumes from the anesthetic. Even she knew ether was highly flammable, so she did not strike a match.

Amy dressed quietly, collected the preacher's clothes, and of course lifted the two bags of cash from under the bed. She was indecisive for seconds before gradually easing off the path of loyalty and onto that of betrayal. She had a lot on her mind, not the least of which was which way to head in the LeBaron. As she closed the door, she smiled at the irony of the plan and how well it had come together.

After two and a half hours, Jimmy was released. The couple had not come and the sheriff had to let him go. Jimmy sat in the front office waiting for Amy, but as the minutes passed, he started to have doubts. A realization was prickling on the edge of his consciousness, itching and drawing him into the idea. It hurt, but it felt right. "Never let them know they've been conned" kept running through his mind.

The story came out in the Marsden and Crossville papers with photos of Jimmy DeVane. His work in Eastern North Carolina was done, but he wondered how far the news would spread up and down the coast. Jimmy poured over plans for revenge and thought that it would be easier to get a lead on Ham than on Amy. He was sure the plan was her idea; Ham couldn't manage something like this.

Jimmy only needed to call another con artist for a loan to get a car; after a few days head start he could be on their trail. There had to be a trail. "Revenge," he whispered. "That stupid, stupid, clever bitch. I'll get my revenge. Jimmy realized that revenge, especially revenge on someone you love, becomes easier once you start. Revenge on Ham was an added benefit."

*****

Her business in Crossville concluded, she now had a little money to spend. Amy drove the LeBaron west, looking to explore new territory. She thought that there would be easy money in the west, especially for an enterprising innocent girl with experience in a big con. There was no trail, no one behind, and only the sweet smell of open air in front.

Amy felt the power of the LeBaron as she passed through Raleigh. As she passed Greensboro, she thought, "Throughout life, my elders told me that I would learn the most from my mistakes. If I could go back, I'd tell them that I've learned the most from my successes."

ABOUT THE AUTHOR

This is my second collection of short stories. Marsden is a rich source for southern personalities and they tell their stories in this collection. Roger, Patrice, and the other characters from **Not Born Here** fill fewer pages but other characters step up with new adventures. I've enjoyed this romp through the southern countryside of North Carolina. The stories are grounded in real life, but any reader who thinks their story is told here is mistaken.

Look for my next project, a novel about a medical student and his unusual gifts: **Faces of a healer.**

The story "Missing Him" won the State Senior games short story competition in North Carolina and is reproduced on their website.

www.ingramcontent.com/pod-product-compliance
Lightning Source LLC
Chambersburg PA
CBHW052006220626
47052CB00004B/1118